Carol Lefevre holds a PhD in Creative Writing from the University of Adelaide, where she is a Visiting Research Fellow. Her first novel *Nights in the Asylum* was shortlisted for the Commonwealth Writers' Prize and won the Nita B. Kibble Award. As well as her non-fiction book *Quiet City: Walking in West Terrace Cemetery*, Carol has published short fiction, journalism, and personal essays. She was the recipient of the 2016 Barbara Hanrahan Fellowship, and is an affiliate member of the J.M. Coetzee Centre for Creative Practice, where she was Writer-in-Residence in 2017. Her most recent book, *The Happiness Glass*, was published by Spinifex Press. Carol lives in Adelaide.

Also by Carol Lefevre

The Happiness Glass (2018)
Quiet City: Walking in West Terrace Cemetery (2016)
If You Were Mine (2008)
Nights in the Asylum (2007)

MURMURATIONS

Carol Lefevre

First published by Spinifex Press, 2020

Spinifex Press Pty Ltd
PO Box 5270, North Geelong, VIC 3215, Australia
PO Box 105, Mission Beach, QLD 4852, Australia

women@spinifexpress.com.au
www.spinifexpress.com.au

Edited by Susan Hawthorne and Pauline Hopkins
Cover design by Deb Snibson, MAPG
Typesetting by Helen Christie, Blue Wren Books
Typeset in Adobe Garamond Pro
Printed by McPherson's Printing Group

For absent friends

'The change in the behavioural state of one animal affects and is affected by that of all other animals in the group, no matter how large the group is.'

"Scale-free Correlations in Starling Flocks"
Proceedings of the National Academy of
Sciences of the USA, June 29, 2010
107 (26) 11865-11870

Contents

After the Island

Emily rose from her seat near the back of the chapel the moment the funeral service was over, and was able to slip outside without having to speak to anyone. There was to be a reception, but she didn't want to eat or drink anything within the crematorium's grounds and among people who worked with Doctor Cleary, or who had known his wife. She didn't know how anyone *could* eat and drink in such circumstances. Then, being the doctor's secretary, people would have come up and spoken to her, for many of them had been surprised at the suddenness of Mrs Cleary's death.

It was late afternoon, with the sky already growing dark. At the bus stop opposite the crematorium gates a cold wind stirred flurries of fallen leaves; no one else was waiting. Emily peeled off a glove and slipped a hand inside her bag to touch her rosary. The beads were made from real rose petals, and the faint perfume they transferred to her fingers was a familiar comfort. Large black birds flapped and shrieked in the treetops further along the road, as Emily said the Our Father and three Hail Marys for the dead woman. The bus appeared then, and a short time later she stepped with relief into the eerily empty interior of the automat.

Emily rarely saw any staff at the self-service café, though she assumed there were people working behind the scenes – there would have to be. The thing she loved about it was that you could fit coins into a slot, turn a knob or press a button, and the glass doors fronting the compartments filled with sandwiches, pieces of pie, and cellophane-wrapped slices of cake, would slide aside, so that you could reach in and take whatever you had chosen. In Emily's life there had been so few opportunities to choose what she would eat, or to choose anything at all, that this simple procedure struck her as the essence of luxury. Also there was no need to make conversation with a waiter, or at the checkout. Of course, the food always had a faintly stale taste and texture from being kept, and if you wanted a hot meal this late in the day you were out of luck.

Emily peeled the soft leather glove from her right hand – the gloves, a parting gift from Sister Lucy, gave her a throb of pleasure each time she put them on or took them off. She stowed it in the pocket of her green coat, pressed a coin into the slot of a vending machine and turned a knob to release a slice of cold apple pie; the pie would do for her evening meal. Emily waited while a machine dripped coffee into a thick white cup. The china here was chunky – less likely to chip, she supposed – though if she ever chose cups and plates for herself she would like something finer, something with a pattern.

Settled at a table with her back to the darkened windows, she started gratefully on the pie. Eating now would save her from the ordeal of tea time at the rooming house, which today, of all days, she wished to avoid. Old Mrs Swithing, her landlady, loved to pick over the details of a funeral – how many were there, what the casket was like, the flowers. Emily imagined the old woman's whiskery chin tilted towards her across the table, the claw-like forefinger hooked in the handle of a bone china cup. The sharp black eyes would bore into her as she awkwardly spooned up vegetable soup, or that dreadful broth that smelled of old dishcloths the cook sometimes inflicted on them, and which Emily believed was a punishment, though what their crimes might have been was beyond knowing.

If she timed it right she could slip upstairs while they were all in the dining room. Then if anyone knocked at her door she could say she had a headache and was going straight to sleep. It was a nuisance being surrounded by people who favoured endless rounds of cards to reading, who watched the worst television programs, or simply sat and nattered about their dull present lives and duller pasts. Emily had a new book from the library; it was about the interpretation of dreams. Reading it would take her mind off things.

Her first weeks as a medical secretary had been alarming. She'd had to learn a complex vocabulary of illnesses and medications; then, after typing letters and notes that documented the relentless creep of various diseases, it wasn't long before she'd begun to experience her own unpleasant symptoms. Emily would finish a letter and then open the medical dictionary – it had been given to her to help with spellings, but she had started using it to research her suspected illnesses. When Sam the cardiologist's secretary caught Emily looking up 'brachycardia', she had burst out laughing.

"Oh, don't worry," she said, "we've all had it. We've had everything! It's a side effect of the job, but it eventually passes."

Sam and Mel and Maureen, the personal assistants of doctors with different specialities, had been typing these letters and notes for years.

"We're survivors of every disease in the dictionary." Mel smiled. "We're practically immortal."

They explained to Emily that having been privy to the intimacies of medical examinations, and personal records, they had now seen and heard everything.

"And some things twice!" Sam gave her snorting laugh.

Being a medical secretary was an education, Maureen said. The things people got up to, you wouldn't believe!

Timidly at first, Emily had begun to join in their conversations in the small, windowless room where they took their morning and afternoon tea breaks, gradually getting to know the other secretaries and their situations – Sam, thick orange foundation applied over white, acne-damaged skin, was in her early thirties, and anxious about having children; Mel, as fine-boned and flighty as a young filly, was grieving the recent death of her father; Maureen, gooseberry-green eyes and a sharp tongue, was homesick for Ireland and regretted leaving it to follow a younger lover. Between them, they had, as they often reminded her, seen everything, but Emily privately thought that none of them had seen anything quite like the death of Mrs Cleary.

At the end of Emily's first week, Sam had found her in the tea room with her hands shaking as she poured herself a mug of strong black tea.

"Is everything all right?" Sam said. She was a farm-bred girl, ruthless in her dealings with the patients but kind and caring with colleagues.

"Yes," Emily said, swallowing hard. "I'm just recovering from an esophagogastrectomy."

"Oh, nasty," Sam said. "Here, have a chocolate digestive."

Emily had bitten into the biscuit and gulped a mouthful of the too-hot tea, puzzled about why she hadn't confided the real reason she was so upset. It hadn't been the complications of the cancer she'd been typing but an abrupt break in the recording, with Doctor Cleary's dry, measured voice interrupted by a series of clicks, and then a hoarse whisper, a woman's voice, in Emily's ear.

If you hear this message, if he doesn't find and delete it, I beg you to listen. My husband is—

Emily had thought she must be hallucinating. She had reversed the tape, tapped replay: there it came again, the same urgent whisper, abruptly cut off. A shiver ran through her. Could it be true? Was it an accident? A joke? At the time, Emily had concluded that the voice must belong to Mrs Cleary, for who else would have access to the doctor's dictation machine?

During the funeral the vicar had said that Mrs Cleary, whose name was Erris, had been fifty-three. A colour photograph at the front of the chapel beside a cascade of orange flowers had been too far away for Emily to gain more than an impression of straight brown hair framing an angular face. In the tea room on the morning of the funeral, Mel had whispered that she'd thought Doctor Cleary's wife could have been older. None of them had seen her in recent times. A weakness for alcohol was mentioned. The longest serving secretary, Glenna, had added that poor Mrs Cleary had let herself go. Emily had supposed she meant that the doctor's wife was overweight, but now she thought that Glenna might have meant something else.

All the specialists at the public hospital worked long hours, and they often dictated their letters at home, even though for confidentiality they were not supposed to. In the weeks following that first encounter with the woman's voice there were other incidents – once, in the middle of a letter about gallstones, the voice broke out in the background, an incoherent babble that dissolved into a howl. The dictation had been halted, the tape rewound a little, and the gallstones letter begun again in a tired voice. But Doctor Cleary hadn't wound the tape back carefully, so that the interruption had not been entirely erased. Twice more there were furtive messages addressed to whoever was typing the doctor's correspondence.

If anything should happen to me, I want you to know that my husband—

Though frightening in its intensity, the voice was well-spoken, and Emily sensed someone who might, under ordinary circumstances, appear calm and capable.

Each time Emily was about to unburden herself to Sam or Mel she was overcome by reluctance. She hardly knew Doctor Cleary, yet his gaunt face, his rounded shoulders tensed like those of a man walking in a rain storm, had roused her sympathy. He had a haunted look, and there was a frailty about his slender wrists that made it difficult to believe he could ever be violent. Nevertheless, Emily had put those tapes into a yellow envelope, and slipped them into an empty pocket in her filing cabinet.

Doctor Cleary had not played the organ at his wife's funeral as he often did when there was a special service in the hospital chapel. Emily had seen him play twice, and had thought how relaxed he looked, leaning forward to read the music while his fingers roamed the keys with a sure touch. Perhaps it was the sound that cheered him, for the measured tread of a hymn could calm even the most agitated soul. Or else it was the pale yellow light falling through the stained glass windows, the intricate red and gold embroidery on the altar cloth.

Having all her life attended twice-daily prayers, Emily had soon established a routine of sitting for a few minutes in the hospital chapel after work, and she sometimes slipped in there during her lunch break. After the island, there were so few quiet places in this new life of hers, and the scent of candle wax, the perfume of the fresh flowers arranged by a team of elderly volunteers, was soothing – if she closed her eyes she could imagine she was at home. Except that there was no Sister Lucy, no Mother Stella Marie. Sister Lucy had warned her that she would be lonely at first, but all these months later the ache of their absence was undiminished.

"Just remember, love, how you are making us proud!" Sister Lucy had said. "And how we will pounce on you with hugs and kisses when you come back to visit!"

Emily had been saving so that she could return at Christmas. The other secretaries were already making holiday plans: Sam's enormous family all converged on the farm; Mel was taking her widowed mother out for Christmas lunch at a posh hotel; Maureen was flying to Ireland, and Sam said she'd be surprised if she ever came back. They'd asked Emily what she was doing, and she'd answered that she would be spending Christmas with family. They knew she came from the island, but she had never yet spoken about the Star of Bethlehem. Mrs Swithing knew, of course, being a distant relative of Mother Stella Marie. Over the years, a steady stream of young men and women from the home had travelled to the mainland; they had stayed at the rooming house at a special rate while they settled into their first jobs and found their feet. To Mrs Swithing's credit, she had never spread it around where they'd come from.

Whenever the little buzz of panic began in her chest, Emily would close her eyes and visualise something she loved at home. Often it was the statue of Mary holding the infant Jesus on the wall of the small courtyard: the pair stood in a boat, for this was Our Lady Star of the Sea. There were nearly always fresh flowers laid across the boat's prow, or at Mary's beautiful plaster feet, sometimes put there by the nuns, but more often left by the wives and children of the island's seagoing fishermen, those silent, salt-roughened men who on sunny days sat mending their nets along the quayside. The faces of the mother and child were exquisitely moulded, and Emily had liked to pretend that this was her own mother, and that the infant Jesus had been modelled on her when she was a baby.

The Star of Bethlehem stood on a spit of land that jutted from the island's rugged coastline. At high tide it was cut off, unless you were prepared to risk the path through the dense belt of blackthorn, and the bracken-laced pines that covered the hills behind. For decades, troubled women had plodded across the wet sand at low tide. On dark mornings, or evenings, drenched with salt spray, they had left newborn babies for the nuns to find, or sometimes handed them over to Mother Stella Marie in broad daylight. When the tide was high a brave and desperate woman might tackle the path through the woods. Sister Lucy thought Emily's mother must have come that way late one night, for the tide had been full when Emily was discovered on the kitchen step at dawn. She'd been well wrapped up, not crying, an infant only a few hours old.

The kindness of those women who had raised her was a light inside Emily – bright and steady as the flames of the votive candles at the foot of the blue-robed Virgin in her niche inside the chapel, or the tall candles on the altar that had never been let go out since the chapel was consecrated. Their affection sustained her on days when her pride in holding down a job, in her precarious independence as a young woman with her own door key, even her pleasure in the books she devoured in the evenings, and the modest luxury of the automat, threatened to collapse. In those moments Emily was herself an island; a girl alone; a girl whose mother had struggled through a pitch-dark wood to deliver her to strangers.

At times the weight of this knowledge threatened to crush her, as it had crushed others who had been raised at the Star of Bethlehem, soft boys like Arthur – who might yet be alive somewhere – bright girls like Linnie, who was not.

Before she died, Doctor Cleary's wife had been admitted to hospital; she had come in through the Emergency Department late at night, and by morning had been moved to Intensive Care. Emily had absorbed this information in silence, sipping strong black tea during the morning break.

"Was there an accident?" Mel asked Sam.

Emily held her breath as she waited for Sam's reply, afraid that what she was about to hear would compel her to take some action she could not yet visualise, though she knew it would mean telling about the tapes.

"I heard it was a brain haemorrhage," Sam said.

Emily breathed again. Surely a brain haemorrhage amounted to natural causes; it was nothing to do with those tapes, and the wild allegations of harm.

When the others returned to their desks Emily sat on for a few minutes in the empty tea room, since she had no letters to type that morning. With her eyes closed she ran through the home things that held her steady: Our Lady in the little boat with her child; the window at the turn of the first floor stairs where you could watch the wooden boats of the island's fishing fleet bravely setting out at dawn and coming home again at dusk. She and Linnie had often squeezed onto the window seat after prayers to watch for their favourites. Emily's was yellow and green, a fishing boat called *Gypsy Dancer*; Linnie's had been red, the *Bonnie Bride*.

The tight feeling came in Emily's chest. Sister Lucy had told her she mustn't dwell on the things that hurt, especially Linnie. So obediently she pushed away the image of *Bonnie Bride* beating towards the harbour on a dull afternoon with the gulls circling, and their warm breath fogging the window glass; she pushed away Linnie's grey eyes with the little bruise-coloured shadows underneath, and the thing she'd said that time.

"You'll dance at my wedding when *I'm* a bonnie bride."

Emily thought instead of the framed scroll on the wall of Mother Stella Marie's study – the Hippocratic Oath that had belonged to her doctor father. He had gone to the First World War and was killed in France after only a week. His death had seemed unbearably tragic at first, but in time Emily had reasoned that at least he hadn't suffered in the trenches for years, only to be killed a week before the end of the war.

Emily had learned to read her first words from studying the scroll while she waited for Mother Stella Marie to finish her work. The nun might be going over the kitchen accounts, or writing to children who had left the Star of Bethlehem and were making their way in the world, as Arthur and Linnie had, as Emily was now.

How remote that prospect had seemed in the days when she lay on the rug sounding out the hand-inked words on the scroll. Since she'd been on the mainland she'd had two letters from Mother Stella Marie. Emily had torn them open in a flush of excitement, and while she was reading they had brought home close. But the feeling had faded, and afterwards home had felt even further away than before. It was not just distant in miles, but obscured somehow, concealed in a fold of time that would be difficult to reach, or even, perhaps, impossible ever to find again. It gave her a little bump of fear in her stomach. Perhaps that's how it had been for Linnie.

In the days after the funeral, Doctor Cleary seemed to Emily to have a new spring in his step. His shoulders were no longer so hunched, and Emily didn't actually hear him whistling, but she saw that his lips were pursed as if he had wanted to whistle but had stopped himself in time.

She remembered how he had sat with his wife in the intensive care ward. Emily had been summoned there to collect his dictation tapes for typing, though he had left them for her at the nurses' station, so she hadn't got even a glimpse of Mrs Cleary. Intensive Care was not as brightly lit as most other hospital wards; it was a tense, ominous place that Emily had been glad to hurry away from.

Eventually, Mrs Cleary had taken a turn for the worse.

"They switched off her life support this morning," Sam said.

"How awful!" There were tears in Mel's soft brown eyes.

Glenna sighed. "In some ways it's a blessing."

Emily had felt the bump in her stomach again. Would it have been Doctor Cleary's decision to turn off the machines that had kept his wife alive? She had waited for Sam or Mel to say something about Glenna's remark that it was a blessing, but neither one of them had spoken.

The latest batch of letters was ready for signature. The doctor surprised Emily by pulling up a chair and signing them on a corner of her desk instead of taking them into his office.

"I'm in a rush, and I have never yet found a mistake in anything you've typed."

He scribbled his initials on the last letter and returned them to her with the flicker of a smile.

He must have been good looking once, Emily thought. What can his life have really been like with his wife – those howls, the accusing whispers?

Before he left he drew another tape from his pocket and handed it to Emily.

"There's no end to sickness, or to letters, I'm afraid," he said. "Luckily these aren't urgent, because I must have forgotten to bring them in for typing, what with everything …"

When he had gone Emily pressed the tape into the machine and pulled on her headphones. She had been typing for perhaps a minute when the doctor's voice was interrupted by the now familiar clicks, and the voice Emily dreaded.

Please, I beg you, if you hear this I need you to tell …

The letter went on again, and then thirty seconds later there was another break.

If you do nothing, and he kills me, it will be your fault!

The voice in Emily's ear was speaking to her directly, its previously pleading tone now pointy with spite. Emily took off the headphones and ejected the tape from the machine. She had done nothing, and Mrs Cleary was dead. Was that her fault? And what action was she to take? If only she could ask Mother Stella Marie, or Sister Lucy, but they seemed so far away, unreachable. It would have been a comfort to have talked to Linnie.

Reluctantly, Emily retrieved the tapes from the filing cabinet, and went next door to Glenna.

Glenna was tidying her desk. "I'm just getting ready for the onslaught after the next clinic," she laughed.

Emily slid onto the visitor's chair and cleared her throat. "Has Doctor Cleary had many secretaries?" she said.

Glenna hooked her long fine hair behind her ears, and her eyes dropped to the tapes in Emily's hands.

"Well … yes," she said. "None of them lasted too long. But sometimes girls don't take to hospital work, or they don't get past the transfer of symptoms stage, and so they look for something else."

"You see ..." Emily hardly knew how to go on, for what she was about to say sounded monstrous in this place where all of their lives were pitched towards helping people battle disease and injury. *It will be your fault!* She had to speak.

Glenna stood up and closed the door. "It's about Mrs Cleary, isn't it?" she said quietly.

Miserably, Emily nodded. "She must have taken his dictating machine out of his pocket." She found it easier to put it this way than to jump right in with the woman's allegations.

"Look, he's a wonderful doctor," Glenna said. "If I ever get cancer, God forbid, I will want to be treated by Doctor Cleary."

"But his wife ..."

"Emily, listen, I'm going to tell you something, but I don't want you to spread it around."

Emily shifted nervously on the chair. "All right," she said.

"Mrs Cleary used to work here in the Blood Clinic. She was a vivacious woman, smart, and good at what she did. But she quit very suddenly, and stayed at home. People said she'd had some kind of breakdown."

"I'd heard she was an alcoholic," Emily said.

"I'm sure. There have been so many stories, some of them quite improbable." Glenna sighed, and her freckled, good-humoured face looked sad. "Things went bad between them. If you ask me it was because they had no children, and it drove Mrs Cleary mad. Anyway, after a while she became involved in a scheme where babies waiting to be adopted were sent to her to be cared for, a sort of short-term fostering."

Emily waited, since Glenna seemed reluctant to go on.

"Didn't that help?" Emily said.

Glenna leaned closer, her face tense and pale. "There were two or three cot deaths," she said.

"Two or three?"

"Three."

The silence in the room rang in Emily's ears. The buzz of panic began in her chest. That woman with the hoarse and frightening voice taking on the care of motherless babies.

"Why did they let her?" Emily whispered.

Glenna shrugged. "On paper she was capable, married to a doctor, the perfect candidate. There were inquests, but nothing could be proved."

Emily thought of Mother Stella Marie's exquisitely moulded eyelids, the kindness and calm that shone from her sea-coloured eyes. She thought of Sister Lucy's cheerful bulk, her sturdy back bent over their rows of summer vegetables, the grace of her blunt grey head bowed in prayer. Over the years there had been one or two nuns she had learned to steer clear of, but those few aside, the sisters had received Emily with joy and had raised her with affection – how fortunate she had been to have fallen into their capable hands. Such a start wasn't any guarantee, of course. Poor Linnie'd had the same, and they had been told she had recited those lines of Saint Patrick's prayer, the ones she would say at night to get herself off to sleep – *Christ in every heart thinking of me, Christ on every tongue speaking to me, Christ in every eye that sees me* – before stepping out of a fourth-floor window at Pullman's shirt factory. She had worked there just over a week.

As the panic picked up its beat in her chest, Emily clung to the image of the scroll on Mother Stella Marie's wall, its ancient oath, and the phrase that leapt out at her now was *Primum non nocere* – First, do no harm. Doctor Cleary would have sworn that oath when he graduated as a doctor. Mother

Stella Marie often said it was a wonderful motto for anyone to live by, and for her sake Emily had resolved to honour it.

There was a knock at the door then, and Sam opened it and stuck her head in.

"I'm going to the shops at lunchtime. Can I bring you anything?"

Glenna smiled and shook her head. "Not unless it's a winning lottery ticket."

The two of them laughed, and under cover of their merriment Emily slid the tapes out of sight into the yellow envelope. After work she would sit in the chapel; she would say a prayer for Linnie, who would never be a bonnie bride, and for Arthur, that he would let them know if he was still alive; she would pray for all the Star of Bethlehem children, past, present, and future, and for herself, too. Then she would take the bus to the automat, and eat there in the quiet.

Little Buddhas Everywhere

The hatpin is a pearl teardrop. Claire picked it up for next to nothing in a charity shop, but it may even be a genuine pearl. You never knew what children would dispose of when a parent died, and vice versa. The dress, too, would have come from some dead woman's wardrobe. Claire presses dry lips together in irritation. Most of the time she manages to suppress such thoughts before they fully surface, because objects hold no memory of the lives they were once part of, and it does not do to dwell. It is too bad that she is forced to shop this way, but only by such economies is she able to keep up any kind of appearance, and keeping up is crucial; it is a full-time job.

Claire has seen what can happen to women who let themselves go, and the fall is so much further than she could ever have imagined when she was in her twenties, or even her thirties. A handful of women she knows have slipped over the edge into that dark abyss, first losing their figures to the empty calories of alcohol, and then losing their faces to the cigarette and suntan years, activities that at the time had seemed so harmless.

Ciggies had been glamorous props – Pall Mall, Dunhill, the rough, French, throat-tearing *Gauloises,* pastel Sobranis, the Black Russians, they had smoked them all. Snake-thin, their limbs had been, and golden, though a tendency to freckle had kept Claire out of the sun, and smoking had made her so sick that she had rarely inhaled. Because later, of course, they learned that tobacco and UV rays were wildly destructive. But by then she and a few of the other women in her circle had lost their husbands – usually to younger women. For some of them the plunge into hardship had been sudden and savage, with one of her old group, Jeanie Tarrant, actually rumoured to be homeless.

Claire turns her ruthless gaze towards the full-length mirror. Never has she allowed herself to avoid this weekly reckoning. For unless you meet age face-on, how can you manage it? Years ago she heard that Erris Cleary smashed up all the mirrors in her house in a drunken rage, including the gilt over-mantle that had been passed down through her husband's family since eighteen-hundred and something. And poor Jeanie never got a full-length mirror in that house she and Rob had stretched themselves to afford in the new estate that had sprung up behind Claire and Tommy's place.

Claire grimaces, remembering her old white-gabled house with its rambling garden. At *Winterbourne* she had entertained her women friends with their children during the day, and with their husbands at night, she had hosted dinner parties for the people from Tommy's work; children's parties, pot luck suppers with two or three other couples, summer barbeques, gatherings around a bonfire with mulled wine and fireworks on Guy Fawkes' night, progressive dinners, curry nights, fondues and fire pots, charity fundraisers. There was that summer they threw the fancy dress party, when Erris turned up as Jay Gatsby in a man's pinstripe suit, and danced all night with Delia Harper. Both their husbands had been furious, and later poor Delia was seen nursing a black eye.

If things went sour there, it was no fault of the house. It had brought her low to leave it, but at least her flat is all paid for, and not too hard to clean or too expensive to run. Poor Jeanie – how proud she had been of her dove-grey and white exterior colour scheme, and of the French windows that overlooked the garden she and Rob had planned but never quite got around to planting.

"I just love the light here!" she'd said when they first moved in, her waif-like figure habitually obliterated under a big shapeless sweater or t-shirt of Rob's.

Jeanie's delight in that gimcrack house had been touching. She used to paint with watercolours, which was maybe why she loved the light. Claire would see her in the mornings, riding past their house on her old black bicycle, slim brown calves pumping the pedals and a scruffy rucksack on her back in which she kept her paints and brushes, her sketchbooks, and sheets of watercolour paper. She would ride for miles to where the streets gradually gave way to farm land, and eventually to the wilderness of Bailey's Wood, only returning to meet the kids from school. Jeanie'd had some of her paintings framed, and hung them on the walls of their house – landscapes, and nature studies, mainly. Claire had bought one from her, and it still hangs in the flat. But back in the day, at drinks parties at Jeanie's and Rob's, when Jeanie was in the kitchen, Claire had overheard people saying that the pictures weren't much good.

The last time Claire had visited Jeanie her walls had been bare, what you could see of them. For after Rob moved out

Jeanie had kept the place closely shuttered, as if the light she'd once loved so much now hurt her eyes. The soft furnishings, Claire recalled, had smelled of dust, of smoke, and fried chicken. Their kids, a boy and a girl, had left home young. Once the support from Rob had petered out Jeanie could no longer afford her cartons of Marlborough Reds. In time she had not been able to cover her utility bills. It was terrifying to think that a woman like that was so reduced, dependant on the dwindling goodwill of her few remaining family and friends. It could happen to any of them.

Erris Cleary, though, is dead, and Claire would say, if anyone asked her, that she is not surprised. It was no surprise, either, when Delia and Roger Harper split. With her hennaed hair and fine white skin, Delia was a flame, and Roger a wet blanket. When they separated, Roger took their boy, and Delia the little girl. She has heard that Roger still lives in the old neighbourhood with a new wife, but no one seems to know what happened to Delia.

Claire turns to the wardrobe, where her dress dangles from the top of the door. Second-hand clothes feel almost new once on a wire hanger under clear plastic, and side-stepping a fate like Jeanie's is worth any amount of distaste for the dress's provenance. It is only women of a certain age who are squeamish about pre-used clothing, she's noticed; young people seem not to care if they walk around in the outfits of the dead. Just last week, Claire overheard one of the granddaughters boasting of a designer dress she'd got at a knockdown price in an Oxfam shop. Juliet, it had been, not her favourite – well, not strictly her granddaughter either, but the eldest of Tommy's children with Rosanna.

That her ex-husband has been married to someone else for so long that one of their offspring shops by herself still amazes

Claire. Eighteen years it has been for Tommy and Rosanna, but thirty-two for Tommy and Claire, so she is still on the winning side. And now it is their golden wedding, or would have been if Tommy had stuck it out with her.

Rosanna doesn't drink or smoke, though privately Claire thinks the UV rays might claim her in the end. Rosanna the runner; Rosanna with the permanently caramel-coloured skin; Rosanna with her spaghetti strap tops beneath which her breasts nestle so casually that they make Claire feel old, and tired, and frumpy, make her feel the full weight of their twenty-one-year age difference. Rosanna works with computers. She understands their complex systems as easily as Claire understands the proportion of sugar, butter, flour, and eggs in a batch of cupcakes or a Victoria sponge. Rosanna uses a sun bed, apparently.

Claire and Tommy are to meet at the Hotel Windsor, where they will sit in their usual spot overlooking the park. The hotel is a little shabby these days, though still respectable, and Claire loves the view from the first floor lounge. She has used the excuse of sorting out the insurance on her flat, for Tommy has always handled their business affairs and he continues to manage things for Claire, even after marrying Rosanna. Claire puts this down to having remained calm and reasonable throughout their split. Knowing Tommy, he would simply have faded from her life if she had kicked up a fuss. As it was, he had negotiated the sale of *Winterbourne* and the purchase of her flat, which she insisted be put into both their names, as the old house had been. It gave her a sense of security, she said, when Tommy had raised his eyebrows. Having his name on the deed to her flat hadn't gone down well with Rosanna, but to Claire it felt as if her ex-husband was still there to look after her if anything went wrong; she felt bolstered by this knowledge, as she had throughout the years of their marriage. Except, of course, when what went wrong was Rosanna.

Though cramped, Claire's flat is in an elegant block in a good suburb, and her ex-husband takes an interest in the ongoing communal matters that arise among the flat owners. Claire could easily manage this herself, but she wants Tommy involved. For when she rings him to discuss this or that small problem, it feels as if they are still together, still a team, despite the fact that he has another wife: Rosanna the feminist, Rosanna the Buddhist, whose politics and religion had not conflicted with stealing another woman's husband.

Feminism caused more than a few casualties among the married couples Claire and Tommy knew. It was a wave that crashed over them, and one or two wives were swept up and carried so far from their suburban homes that they could find no way back. There was Annie Darkley, who after reading *The Feminine Mystique* had lurched to her feet in the middle of a dinner party to announce that she was no longer prepared to clean a bathroom where three males went to piss. She'd had too much to drink, but still. The silence at the table had frightened Claire, though privately she had sympathised. Not long afterwards, Annie had walked out on her husband and their two boys. Claire heard she'd sold her engagement ring and flown to India, 'to find herself' as people said then. Later, stories filtered back of a gang rape in Goa, of Annie's parents flying out to bring her home, and of the need for ongoing psychiatric care.

After the Annie Darkley scandal, Claire had thought the next to go would be that fawn-like Fiona Padwick. She and her husband Danny had seemed locked in a private struggle, the nature of which Clare could only guess. But they had stuck it out, or they had up until that time a few years back when she bumped into them out Christmas shopping. Danny had put on an alarming amount of weight; Fiona was still as wary as a deer about to bolt, but there they were, buying fancy cheeses together.

Whenever Claire thinks about Fiona Padwick and Annie Darkley she understands her own ambivalence towards the women's movement. Women deserve equal pay for equal work, no question, but it is not as if men are ever going to shoulder their share of the housework and child-rearing. And with a soft man like Tommy, Claire had known she would get more with honey than with vinegar: the one bit of wisdom she had been able to glean from her mother. Perhaps women like Annie, who were borne away on the feminist wave, were already chaffing within their marriages, whereas Claire, after a difficult childhood, had crept into matrimony like a hermit crab into an empty shell. She had felt protected, and had chosen to manage Tommy rather than to make demands. Which is why he is still in her life, even if he is married to someone else.

Rosanna, though, has negotiated a fairer division of labour. Tommy works around the house. He would even get up in the night to their children when they were small – something he never did for Claire after Martin was born. Recoiling from her son's unbidden appearance in her thoughts, Claire remembers the first time she stayed with Tommy and Rosanna – it was that terrible winter when she'd had pneumonia, and was too weak to shop or cook for herself – and how astonished she had been to see Tommy vacuuming the living room. She still wonders what he had to promise Rosanna so that she could stay. Their daughters had been small, that first time, and when Tommy brought her home he had introduced her to Penny and Juliet as 'Aunty Claire', having already warned her that Rosanna thought the girls far too young to understand that Claire had once been married to their father.

There had been small Buddhas ranged along the window-sills in the guest bedroom. Claire always remembers this with a wry smile, for Rosanna's Buddhism seems an affectation, like the cigarettes Claire once posed with at parties but didn't inhale. When the door had closed behind Tommy she had picked up the little resin figures, one by one. Some were slender, meditating with half closed eyes, while others had broad bald heads and chubby bellies – the fat ones all seemed to be either laughing or sleeping. Of the slender figures, some held their hands in prayer, some pointing to the earth. One held a bowl in his lap. One held a lotus flower. Their arrangement in the room where she would sleep had struck Claire as talismanic: Rosanna was protecting her household against Claire's evil eye.

As if to support this theory, when Aunty Claire's presence at Christmases and birthdays had become a ritual the children insisted upon, and looked forward to, Claire noticed that the Buddhas had multiplied, that there were, in fact, little Buddhas everywhere, even on the windowsill in the downstairs powder room, and resting along the tops of door frames – these latter were made of white plaster, so that you hardly noticed them against Rosanna's stark white walls. On the sill above the kitchen sink was a miniature altar. That Buddha received daily offerings – cones of incense, rose petals, flower heads floating in a shallow dish. Once, Claire had seen half a peach balanced in the Buddha's lap.

Tommy's youngest, Penny, had known all their names, and she would move along the windowsills, solemnly reciting them for Claire.

"This is the Medicine Buddha, see, with the bowl of herbs? And this one is the Happy Buddha; this, the Teaching Buddha …"

From Penny, Claire learned that there were Begging Buddhas, and Laughing Buddhas; there were Preventing the Relatives from Fighting Buddhas, and Nirvana Buddhas. At Christmas, and sometimes on Penny's birthday when she is able to wangle an invitation, Claire looks forward to seeing how many more Buddhas Rosanna has crammed into their house.

It is a bit of luck the insurance has fallen due, so that there is something to discuss with Tommy. Once he realises the significance of the date she feels sure he will indulge her in a small, private celebration. In her handbag she has a gift already wrapped – gold cufflinks, each set with a small ruby. To afford them, Claire has tightened her belt even further than usual. She wants to see her husband's face when he realises she has gone to some trouble for him; she wants to see that dimple that flashes in his left cheek when he feels a surge of affection for her – for even now it still sometimes surfaces. It is a small thing, this relic of their shared past, but it seems to say to Claire that often when you think something precious has been lost it has really only been mislaid.

She pulls the dress over her head, and fumbles her arms into the sleeves. Once, when she and Tommy met at the hotel not long after they were divorced, Claire had told him that autumn had always been her favourite season. She had gestured towards the window, where tawny leaves were being tossed and teased by the wind. There was still some gold left in her, she'd said, for the right person. Claire had truly felt that then, and sometimes felt it still. Tommy had laughed, rather nastily, she'd thought. He had made a remark about her hair, which she had

25

been experimenting with growing out grey – another economy – and after that she had hurried back to the hairdresser. What was it Tommy had said? Claire has banished his exact words to some dim, outer sphere of memory, though the sense of hurt remains.

The dress fits snugly over her hips, raspberry lace, and even though she has had to remove the stained silk rose at the neck it still looks a million dollars because, if nothing else, she has kept her figure. When Claire has finished putting on her face – not too much, because Tommy doesn't like overly made-up women – she steps into her shoes, and shrugs on her coat, bracing her shoulders against the weight of it.

"There!" It isn't far to the hotel, but she will take a taxi, and to hell with the expense.

Tom Delaney could swear he is being strangled by invisible hands. He slips the top button of his shirt and wrenches at the knot of his tie, loosening it a little, taking in a big gulp of the early evening air that is greasy with fast-food smells and exhaust fumes. Around him, people are streaming out of the glass fronts of office buildings, roaring past in their cars, rushing towards whatever awaits them, while he hovers at this pedestrian crossing, cursing himself for agreeing to meet Claire.

When she rang him he had wanted to scream. The thought of sitting down with her in that bloody hotel she likes had felt like the last straw to a camel. But he'd agreed to go, and now that the hour has arrived he feels so unsettled that he wonders whether he should stop at a bar and take a steadying drink. The light turns green, and he lunges forward, resolved to get it over with.

When he searches his mind for some way to begin the conversation, the sensation of being strangled returns: in the lobby of the Windsor Hotel Tom pulls off his tie, rolls it up and shoves it into his jacket pocket. He imagines Claire's face when she sees him emerge from the lift without it, and with his shirt undone. She won't say anything, but he will see the tightening of her mouth that makes her look like her mother, the icy gleam that enters her clear grey eyes from who knows what light source. These are the outward expressions of her displeasure. Christ, it is almost unnatural, Claire's ability to control her feelings, and part of him admires her for it, her resolute grace, her implacable dignity. But another part believes Claire's reticence is the reason he fell so hard for Rosanna. Claire could never let herself go, not in bed, not on the few occasions she'd drunk too many cocktails, not even – and this was hardest to believe – in those desperate days after they lost Martin.

Only once has he known Claire give way to tears, and fucking hell if it wasn't because they'd had to re-home their cat, Sixpence. He'd had to explain to her that the charter of the flats excluded pets. So they'd taken the cat to someone Claire knew – she had been Martin's friend – Lizbie bloody Menick, or Lizbie the Manic, as he'd thought of her, which had been a bit unkind, because she was really just an oddball kid. Lizbie had stayed with them once when she had nowhere to go – anyway, Sixpence had no sooner moved in with her than she'd given birth to a single kitten. Claire swore she hadn't known Sixpence was pregnant, but Jesus Christ, the fuss there'd been with Lizbie!

He and Claire had been in the midst of the divorce, and although on the surface all was calm, they had really been like a pair of ducks on a pond, paddling madly underwater. He had wanted to shout at Lizbie that her place was a complete fucking shit heap, to which an extra cat would make no difference, and that it was no wonder her drip of a husband had topped himself. In the end, when the kitten was weaned he had taken it home. Rosanna had balked at keeping a litter tray in the laundry, but she'd relented when he'd explained about Claire, and crazy-as-bat-shit Lizbie.

Sometimes he wonders how different his life would be now if he hadn't found Rosanna before Martin discovered drugs. He doubts he would have had the guts to deal Claire a second blow, but by then it was all a done deal; they had started the divorce. But yeah, Claire had cried when she handed over Sixpence, yet she was dry-eyed after they heard their son was dead of a heroin overdose. Tom often wonders what a psych would make of that. Otherwise, you couldn't fault her.

Rosanna has plenty to say, of course, mostly about the way that, over the years, Claire has hot-wired herself into their lives. It is true that he sometimes feels his ex-wife's reasonableness is designed to keep him distracted while her tentacles fasten more tightly around his throat. Like that time she claimed to have had pneumonia: personally, he still gives her the benefit of the doubt, but Rosanna has never believed she was as ill as she said. And then somehow she'd started spending Christmases with them. Rosanna had only asked that Claire stop calling him Tommy; it made him sound like a teenager, she said, or some spiv who would hang about at race tracks, losing money. But Tom knew it would do no good to raise it with Claire, so he hadn't, and after a while Rosanna had stopped rolling her eyes every time.

The children had taken to her, especially Penny. Claire had taught them to bake gingerbread men and to knit long striped scarves – he didn't know whether that had made her presence more bearable for Rosanna or whether she had taken it as a criticism.

The choking sensation returns as he enters the lift, and Tom slips another button of his shirt and sucks in air. The thing about that episode with Lizbie and the cat was that it had happened on the day they'd had to deal with Martin's bedroom. For the two years after he died they had barely opened the door, but the divorce, and the sale of the house, had forced them to sort through his belongings. Tom had been amazed, and then stricken, at how little their son had owned – a couple of second-hand guitars and amplifiers, books from childhood, clothes too worn to give to charity. There were stacks of records by artists you'd never heard of. And in the bottom of his wardrobe, one pair of shoes. He remembers standing in the middle of that sparely furnished room, hot with shame at the realisation that their only son had been living his life in a single pair of scuffed black brogues. He had wept then, and later Claire had cried over the cat, but he reckons a psych would say they were both crying for the same reason.

The first floor lounge of the Windsor has a faded blue carpet, yellow walls and darker yellow curtains that don't quite touch the floor. There are tub chairs, and one square blue sofa in front of the window, and Claire sighs her relief when she sees the sofa is vacant. She settles in but drapes her coat around her shoulders, for a chill falls from the plate glass window. Outside, trees heave and subside in a breathing motion that reminds her of the ocean. When a waiter appears, she explains that she would like a small club soda while she waits for her husband. For years now, with strangers, she has given up explaining that they are divorced. She is taking her first sip when the lift doors part, and Tommy walks towards her.

Claire feels that lift of gladness the sight of him always brings. She likes the way he wears his clothes, for Tommy is not one of those men whose body strains at the cloth of his shirt, or his trousers. He gained a pound or two in his middle years, it's true, but his height ensures a degree of elegance. However, Tommy Delaney is not looking his best this evening, and Claire notes shadows under his eyes, and in the hollows of his cheeks. His hair needs a trim, too, and he is without his tie. In the month since she last saw him, Tommy seems to have aged.

"Claire," he says. "Am I late?"

She shakes her head and smiles. Even his voice sounds different; perhaps he is getting a cold.

Tommy thrusts a hand into his right trouser pocket and jingles coins, then looks away to where the waiter is drifting towards them from the bar. Claire remembers the jingling as a nervous habit.

"To be honest, I haven't much time." He draws up a tub chair and sits facing her. "There's always time for a gin and tonic, though. What about you?"

"Yes, please," she says, though she had anticipated something more celebratory.

She watches her husband order. How often have they entered cafes, restaurants, and country pubs together? Tommy's profile hovering at the counter, or speaking to a waiter, is as familiar to Claire as the back of her own hand.

"Well," he says, once they've taken their first sips of gin, "I've rung around, and I think you should stick with the same insurance company."

"It was kind of you to do that for me," she murmurs.

He swirls the ice in his glass and looks past her to the window. "It was no trouble."

Claire is reaching into her handbag for the gift, when Tommy suddenly sucks in a breath and leans towards her.

"Bit of bad news, I'm afraid, Claire."

"Oh?" She withdraws her hand from the bag and curls it in her lap.

Tommy rubs at his throat. "Rosanna had a mammogram," he says. "Something showed up."

A mammogram? Those breasts, so poised beneath singlet tops and strapless summer dresses?

"Rosie's going for surgery, both sides. It's drastic, of course, but the safest option."

Claire sees two small brown breasts, lying together in a stainless steel kidney bowl. There is a sensation in her own breasts; a pulsing there, penetrating as a sonar beep. The pulse becomes painful as she thinks: Rosanna. Has. Breast. Cancer. That sun bed. Those UV rays. To Claire's surprise, there is no sense of triumph, but a muted, unexpected grief.

Tommy clears his throat, and his face is flushed. "The thing is, we can't have you to stay this Christmas," he says. "In fact, Rosanna and I are spending Christmas in Hawaii."

"Hawaii?" Who goes to Hawaii when they have cancer?

"Rosanna wants to get away, just the two of us."

"But Juliet, and Penny."

Tommy shifts in his chair. "Juliet is going on holiday with friends. It's been booked for a year, and Rosanna thinks she should go ahead."

Claire's mind is working so slowly now. "Penny must be terribly upset."

"Penny has refused to go to Hawaii," Tommy says, "because of the cat."

Claire remembers that their cat has been having treatment for something that has cost thousands in veterinary fees.

Tommy is rubbing at his throat again. "Twopence is old, and Penny thinks she'll die if she's sent to board."

Claire absorbs this information in silence.

"Penny asked if she could stay with you," Tommy says quietly.

"With me? At the flat? But they don't allow cats."

"It's *Penny* who wants to spend Christmas with you," Tommy says. "And I think I could fix things for Twopence with the admin committee. If not, you could move in to our place."

Penny is what, fifteen? How do you make a fifteen-year-old do anything they don't want to do? There are ways, Claire supposes, and Rosanna knows them all. She can only conclude that Rosanna wants a break; she wants to go away, having had a double mastectomy, to recuperate in a hotel room in Hawaii. It is madness!

In the silence that has fallen between them, Claire feels something melting, dripping. She looks down the front of her dress to see whether she has accidentally spilled the gin, but the lace is spotless.

"I'm sorry," Tommy says.

"Sorry?"

"Well," he glances out at the swaying treetops, "I know you hate it when everything shuts down over the holidays."

Claire nods. Martin's absence haunts her then, all the bright promise of his life extinguished by the prick of a needle, as in some grotesquely twisted fairy tale.

"But I won't be alone," she says. "There'll be Penny, and Twopence." Claire's smile is tremulous, and then firms as she mentally repeats what she's just said.

The dimple in Tommy's left cheek flashes once at Claire.

"I wasn't counting on you being willing to take them, he says. "But if you will, then ..."

The melting inside her is an actual flow now rather than the dripping. Penny has no useful extended family, for Rosanna is an only child whose parents died years ago; Tommy's mother bolted with a real estate agent to Canada when he was still married to Claire, and his father, an ancient curmudgeon who detests children, lives in a distant city. So Claire has played grandmother to Penny, and to some extent Juliet, though they both still call her Aunty. She supposes it is odd for children to be close with their father's ex-wife, but she will not fret about this.

There will be a tree, a small one, shining in the window of her flat, and presents to wrap and unwrap, and carol singing on the television. Visualising this unexpected scene, Claire experiences the weird shift in perception that sometimes comes over her when she stays with Tommy and Rosanna. It might begin with Penny leaning against her while she shows her how to hold her knitting needles, and then the cat might start to purr on the sofa beside them – the cat that is the image of her old cat, Sixpence, who is forever linked in Claire's mind with the white-gabled house of her early marriage. Then, Claire might look up and see Tommy walking towards her with a drink, and she feels as if she has fallen into another version of their life, the life they *might* have lived.

They descend together in the lift. Tommy wants to put her into a taxi outside the Windsor, but Claire insists that she will walk.

"It's late night shopping, still plenty of people about," she says.

He pecks at her cheek. "I'll tell Penny, then," he says, "about Christmas."

"Oh, absolutely! And Tommy," she squeezes his hand, "I'm so sorry about Rosanna."

He manages a tight smile. "Thank you. It will be fine, I know it will."

And with any luck it will be fine, for Rosanna is still relatively young, and strong. Claire watches him walk to the corner, his shoulders hunched in a way that is new to her, and when he is out of sight she remembers that she didn't give him the cufflinks.

Claire passes a row of brightly lit shops, a café, a smart boutique. In the next block, the greengrocer has boxes piled with fruit and vegetables on the pavement. The shop beside it, owned by a Pakistani family, sells everything from packets of incense to handwoven rugs, and knitwear from Nepal. Claire has bought cones of incense here for Rosanna and silk scarves for herself.

Now, peering into the crowded window, she sees a small brass Buddha. Inside, there are more Buddhas, of all shapes and sizes. She chooses an exquisite Medicine Buddha carved from smooth, dark wood; she will wrap this in beautiful paper and give it to Rosanna. Then she picks out the Laughing Buddha, the Sleeping Buddha, and Serenity Buddha, and others whose names she does not know. She will not arrange these in the room where Penny will sleep with her aged cat, but in the sitting room, tucked into the pine garland she plans to drape over the mantelpiece. Penny will tell her the names of these little Buddhas, as they protect and preserve her mother, as they preside over these precious days of unlooked-for pleasure that in another version of their lives belong to Claire.

Evening All Afternoon

Fiona was crumpling newspaper to set the fire when the doorbell shrilled. She glanced at the clock, and considered lying doggo. It was half-past two on one of those dark Sunday afternoons when the house smelled of chimneys and hidden damp, and for the past hour she had been trying not to give in to gloom. The mood that tugged at her was as familiar as breath; it was not the kind that welcomed company. She looked around the first-floor sitting room, which in the aftermath of the ringing felt unnaturally quiet. Its tall unshuttered windows framed lengths of bruise-coloured sky, its lamps were still unlit, and everything looked slightly insubstantial in the dimness. From the street it would appear as if no one was home; Fiona was prepared to sit it out. Then she heard Pippa's footsteps hurrying down, and with a sigh she rose from where she had been crouching on the hearthrug.

Barry Darkley was standing in the open doorway. His two boys were with him, the youngest, Clem, peering under his father's arm with that rabbit-in-the-headlights look Fiona so disliked, though to feel that way about a small child, she knew, was beyond shameful. The Darkleys lived in an old house surrounded by muddy, gorse-bound fields that petered out towards the coast, and Barry's waxed jacket and tweed cap smelled of wet leaves and wood smoke when he stooped to kiss Fiona's cheek.

She might have known it would be Barry. He was one of the few people who dropped in uninvited, usually when he'd been charged with getting the boys out of the house for a few hours to give Annie a break.

"We're off for a trot around the lake," he said. "Wondered if you and Pippa would like to come?"

"Dan's not in," Fiona said, "otherwise I'm sure he'd have been up for a walk."

Barry's high forehead wrinkled, and the smile he beamed at her seemed forced, while his eyes – small and very blue in his long pale face – appeared to be pleading with Fiona.

When she hesitated, Pippa took her hand and tugged.

"Oh, can we, Mum? Please!"

Fiona peered past Barry into the chilly street, at the clouds that looked to be resting on the hill behind the houses opposite. The winter afternoon was muted, the colour of everything like the colour of old pewter.

"I don't think it's going to rain." Barry's voice was hearty, and just a touch wheedling.

"No …" Fiona thought regretfully of the unlit fire upstairs, the book she had abandoned face down on the sofa. The last thing she wanted was to walk in the park with its stark leafless trees and the sullen expanse of the boating lake, which even in summer she found dank and unappealing. But Pippa was wriggling with excitement, so Fiona fetched their coats; she hunted for her keys, and money in case the kiosk in the park was open. They might get a paper cup of that bitter filter coffee, she supposed, and although it was cold, the children would demand ice cream.

Fiona shut the front door, and they walked to the turnoff to the park, she and Barry side by side on the narrow footpath and Pippa and the two boys galloping ahead.

"Thanks for coming," Barry said, his voice thick with unexpected emotion. "I could see you didn't really want to be out in the cold."

Fiona glanced up at him in surprise. With the children out of earshot all the heartiness had drained from Barry's demeanour, and he looked, well he looked as if he were about to cry.

"Is something wrong?" she said.

With the backs of his fingers he flicked nervously at his neck, and at the underneath of his chin, where a rash had spread upwards from his collar.

"Annie's leaving me," he said. "She's going this afternoon."

Fiona gaped at him. "What, for good?"

Barry's forward movement ground to a halt, and they stood facing each other on the path.

"The thing is …" he raked his fingers once more over his reddened neck, "I haven't told the boys."

Fiona's shocked gaze swung from Barry's chaffed skin to the children, who had reached the little hump-backed bridge at the entrance to the walkway that circled the boating lake. Clem and Griff were leaning out over the railing, dropping sticks into the water; Pippa's laughter drifted back to where Fiona stood with their father.

"But surely Annie has prepared them?" Fiona said.

Barry shook his head; he was rummaging in his coat pocket for a handkerchief. "Annie couldn't bring herself to say anything," he said. "I'm afraid it's a complete shambles."

Fiona hadn't seen Annie for months, but she'd heard a rumour that she and Barry were going through a difficult time. There had been a dinner party where Annie had said provocative things, feminist things, apparently. Fiona and Dan hadn't been able to find a babysitter that night, and later, when they'd heard about the fuss, Fiona had been glad to have missed it. People said Annie'd had too much to drink, which Fiona doubted: Annie was a green tea and juicing enthusiast.

"Annie's organised someone with a trailer," Barry said. "She's taking some furniture that belonged to her grandmother. Griff and Clem have no idea …"

"The children are waiting for us to catch up," Fiona murmured, "we'd better go on."

They walked towards the bridge in silence, and Fiona thought of the last time she had seen Annie.

They had sat on a bench in the park watching their children scramble over the play equipment. It had been the tail end of the summer, with a breath of autumn in the late-afternoon air, and it was that smokiness of the season turning, the prospect of the winter to come, that had plunged Fiona into one of her blackest-ever bouts of homesickness.

Of the women they knew, she and Annie were the only ones who were living far from the places where they had been raised. In Fiona's case, she had been forced to relocate because of Dan's work; Annie had always accepted she would live wherever Barry decided. Fiona had fretted from the first, but Annie had seemed resigned, even pleased, to have settled in a place so distant from her family. Barry had once confided to Dan that it wasn't up to much, the place Annie had come from. Dan and Fiona had agreed that Barry was a bit of a snob.

That afternoon at the park, Fiona had stared at the patch of scuffed grass at their feet and poured out how it broke her heart to watch Pippa growing up without family – at home there were grandparents, aunties and uncles, small cousins, the offspring of old school friends. Was it unrealistic to want these permanent ties for Pippa? Besides, if she did not grow up there, when she went back it would always be as a visitor. Annie had sat twiddling the long dark braid of hair that reached to her lap, while Fiona had plunged into a maudlin, self-indulgent attack of melancholy.

She had hated this place from the start, hated its weather, and the way people talked, hated its ugly houses, and the shapes of the trees; she hated the way locals stuck together, the way they were always reminding you that you didn't belong, that you would never be one of them, however long you stayed; she hated when they banged on about the natural beauty of the place when honestly it was bleak, and much of it rundown, and all of it desperately behind the times. What she dreaded most, she'd said, was being stuck here until she was old, or dying and being buried here, trapped forever in its cold and hostile soil. Annie's face had crumpled at that, and Fiona saw that she had never yet looked ahead to her own mortality, never envisaged dying and being buried among virtual strangers.

"If it makes you so unhappy, you should go," Annie had said, her eyes blurred by tears.

And now it was Annie who was going – Annie with her torrent of hair and her home-baked biscuits, her belief in the benefits of yoga, and her interest in astrology.

"I'm almost sure there's someone else," Barry said. "Annie says there isn't, but there has to be."

He darted a quick assessing glance at Fiona, as if to catch her out in some guilty knowledge of his wife's infidelity. But if Annie had been having an affair, she hadn't taken Fiona into her confidence. Fiona shook her head, baffled. Already her mind had leapt ahead to the moment when Barry and the boys would arrive home, and the desolation of entering the dark empty house, with its spaces where, when they had left it, familiar pieces of furniture had stood. Their mother would not be there to tuck them into bed, perhaps for the first time in their lives.

"You'd better stay for tea," Fiona said faintly.

Barry had found his handkerchief, and blew his nose. "The boys would love that," he said.

For all the good it would do, thought Fiona, because they would have to go home at some point. But at least she could see to it that the children ate, that they wouldn't have to confront their grief on empty stomachs.

Fiona and Dan had survived their own crisis. It had been the usual trouble: Fiona's homesickness, Dan's stubborn refusal to believe their lives would be different if they moved. Weren't his parents good enough grandparents for Pippa? And then there was the question of making a living – Dan was deep into a business venture with his father. He was an only child. How was he to walk away from a family company he had helped establish? Fiona had felt beaten.

And then had come one of those moments where suddenly everything was in flux: they had sold their house and not yet bought a new one. Fiona said she would take Pippa and go back home. She had gambled on the strength of their marriage, and on Dan being so unhappy without them that he would follow. In her muddled mind she had thought that somehow it would all work out. Instead, she had ended up where she longed to be, but more miserable than she had ever thought possible.

The prospect of living alone, of raising Pippa alone, had been daunting. Their separation had become messy, with her family urging her to stay, and Dan remaining firm. Friends like Annie Darkley and Erris Cleary had assumed she'd gone back home for a break, that she was catching some winter sun. Erris had sent a postcard and signed it with a silly sketch of a group of them drinking coffee under a striped café awning in their overcoats; an empty chair bore Fiona's name. *P.S. Summer's coming, hurry back!*

Fiona had never told a soul about her loneliness, more piercing even than homesickness, or about the hours she'd spent crying on the phone to Dan before she'd finally returned. Now she wondered guiltily whether she had gone too far that afternoon in the park with Annie, and whether she had infected her with her own restlessness.

She and Barry walked halfway around the lake, Fiona keeping her eyes from its scum-flecked water, only to find the kiosk closed: *Shut due to a family funeral. We regret any inconvenience to our customers.* Fiona winced under her coat and wrapped her scarf more firmly. After all, they would not have to drink the stale filter coffee; the children would not eat ice cream, though once they saw that the kiosk wasn't open they lost interest.

The clouds had settled into the dark mass of the pines behind the park. A breeze flicked little wavelets over the surface of the lake, and its shallow water slapped the concrete sides with a sad sloshing sound. Fiona thought of the fire she would light as soon as they got in, and of what to give the children for their tea. Her eyes followed the two boys, their small bodies hurtling on into the grey afternoon, and she imagined Annie with her grandmother's chiffonier roped onto a trailer. Where on earth would she take it?

41

There was a shepherd's pie in the freezer. For dessert, the remains of a carrot cake, and bowls of vanilla ice cream, and squares of milk chocolate. The Darkley boys ate everything; their faces in the lamp-light were relaxed, not yet shocked or contorted by grief. Fiona could hardly bear to look at them.

Barry kept up a stream of chatter, and Fiona was relieved when Dan rolled in.

"Well! What a gathering!" He poured himself and Barry a glass of wine from an already opened bottle, and sat at the end of the table.

Relieved of the responsibility of making conversation, Fiona retreated to the kitchen and slowly began to load the dishwasher.

When Dan came in for more wine he saw her face. "What's up?" he said.

In a low-pitched voice, she told him.

"Jesus! Really?"

The children had finished eating and begun a boisterous game; their small socked feet thudded up and down the stairs. Barry, white-faced, announced that he would take them home before the game got out of hand.

"Wait, stay for coffee," Fiona urged.

She found a packet of marshmallows and showed the children how to toast them on the fire using skewers. The three adults lingered over coffee. It had begun to rain, and the sound of it beating against the window glass made the room and everything in it seem snug and secure, as if everything would be all right for as long as they remained safe within its sheltered warmth. The flames cast a golden blush on the children's hands, and on their faces that were sticky with melted marshmallow. It burnished the boys' blonde heads, and Fiona saw that beneath the fine silky hair their skulls were as fragile as new-laid eggs, and perhaps as strong. She thought of the house that waited for them on the edge of the darkened fields, its front door locked, its windows unlit, its rooms muffling the squalling wind and rain. While somewhere, in a room she could not envisage, Annie's grandmother's chiffonier carried in its recesses dust gathered over the years of Annie's and Barry's marriage; in its diligently polished surfaces, dormant reflections of lighted birthday candles and strings of Christmas lights, of all the ordinary winter evenings when they had gathered around the fire as a family.

Barry put down his empty coffee cup, and turned to Fiona. "Well … it's been a lovely afternoon."

"Is there anything we can do?" she said. In her mind rose the image of the three of them in the car, the approach to the house. When would Barry tell them? When would the knowledge of their mother's absence finally penetrate those fragile skulls? Barry shook his head. His eyes were moist as he scratched at his neck.

"C'mon, boys," he said, "it's time."

Glory Days

Lizbie had been out walking after a fight with her mother, plunging along unfamiliar streets, fizzing with fury, and adamant that she was never going home. And then music drifted from a house she was passing, an acoustic guitar, and two voices fused in a loosely phrased yet melting harmony: the beauty of it had brought her to a standstill. The house had a white front gate; *Winterbourne* was written on it in crisp black letters. She could see white gables, a black front door with a decorative fanlight, but the bulk of the house was concealed from the street by a severely clipped, ten-foot cypress hedge. She had stood listening, inhaling the cypress's sharp, green, medicinal scent.

The voices were male – young men, by the sound of them; the guitar playing was understated and fluid. When they finished she had clapped, a little shower of applause to let them know that what they were doing was cool. She'd been about to walk on when the gate opened – they'd come out to see who was eavesdropping – and there she was, Lizbie Menick, in her ripped shorts and cowboy boots, and her semi-see-through cheesecloth blouse, with the hair her mother liked to call 'bay red' tumbling over her shoulders.

That was how she'd met Marty Delaney and Griff Darkley. Marty was the guitarist and songwriter; Griff's high, angelic voice could make you weep, and he was handy on bass, and two or three other instruments. Lizbie's tremulous contralto had found a space between them, and eventually they had let her sing with them at gigs, working up a few *a capella* pieces to show off the harmonies. Their repertoire was based around covers of popular songs, but when they really shone, in Lizbie's opinion, was when they played Marty's originals. For a while she believed she had stumbled into her perfect life.

The shrink never looks at her watch, but Lizbie suspects there is a clock somewhere in the room, one without a tick. She is aware of time being measured; it is pointless, really, this so-called talking cure. In the hours she has spent here, the backs of her knees sticking to the puffy leather of one of those ugly recliner chairs all psychiatrists keep for their clients, this shrink, like others she has seen, has never said anything that has helped her get through her days. They have excavated Lizbie's childhood right down to the fact that she was named after a poem by Thomas Hardy. Sometimes Lizbie wants to shake the woman. Other times she wants to shock her.

"Of course, Marty and Griff both wanted to fuck me."

The shrink doesn't bat an eyelid; she appears to Lizbie to be made of something like the materials that must be used to quake proof tall buildings.

"And which of them did you want?" The therapist's voice is mild, her grey eyes unblinking behind steel-rimmed glasses.

"I wanted them both," Lizbie says.

For a moment she sees them on the verandah where they had been playing that Sunday morning – Marty with no shoes, no shirt, a length of blue batik cloth clinging to his narrow hips and dark hair falling into his eyes, Griff with his silky blonde beard and his lazy smile.

"They were …" she feels her composure dissolving, and draws in breath, "… exquisite. They were exquisite human beings, each in their different ways," she says. "I slept with both of them, of course, but it was Griff I married."

But her session is over. It never matters where they have got to; when the hour is up the shrink rises from her chair and calls time. A part of Lizbie resents this, and another part doesn't blame her: imagine listening all day to people's fucked up lives, the disasters they've brought upon themselves and the shit that fate has stuck in their path for them to slip arse over kite on. As she pays at the reception desk, Lizbie thinks she won't come again. Because what point is there in throwing good money after bad when Marty and Griff are gone, and her perfect life has turned out a shipwreck. This woman she pays to listen to her knows less than she does. Lizbie tells herself she will just have to survive until it is all over for her, too, and the sooner the better.

Before she fell in love with Marty, Lizbie had fallen for his house. It was that first glimpse of *Winterbourne*, its white gables, and the black door with its fanlight like half a snowflake. Although it was really just a large suburban home, in her imagination it had been a lighthouse, set steadfast upon a rock, impervious to storms, a fixed point in the tilting world. The thing she'd loved most was that it was always immaculate, as if elves emerged at night to dust and polish, and whisk everything into place, like in that fairy tale about the shoemaker.

No such elves favoured her own house – for while her mother could argue all day long against see-through blouses and push-up bras for teens, she couldn't keep a kitchen or a bathroom clean. In Lizbie's opinion, her mother should cull ninety per cent of her belongings and give what remained a thorough scrub. And she was damned if she was going to become a midnight elf all the while her ma sat festering in that decrepit garden shed she called her 'Writing Room', pecking away at her portable typewriter.

Marty's mother was the one who kept everything shipshape. Lizbie was a bit afraid of Claire Delaney, but she revered her impeccably laundered table linen, her pressed pillowcases and sheets that smelled of fabric softener when you shook them out to put them on the bed. She loved her pantry with its shelves of bottled plums and peaches, and jars of chutney and jam, all made from fruit trees in the garden. Claire was a gold standard housekeeper; there was never a rush to clean up because people were coming over, and there were people in that house every weekend of the year.

Marty claimed his mother had entertained when he was a kid so that he could appear to have friends.

"She's always been terrified I wouldn't turn out normal," he said, giving his smoky laugh.

Marty had been a solitary child, and hadn't taken to any of the children who came to the house with their parents, until he met Griff. Marty and Griff had been solid ever since. After Griff's mother Annie left home, or as Griff always put it in that dry, throw-away tone he reserved for speaking about her, 'After Ma got Liberated', he and his younger brother Clem had stayed at *Winterbourne* while their father chased Annie down and tried to coax her home. Lizbie often wondered how different all their lives might have been if he had succeeded.

But Annie Darkley had bolted to a commune in India she'd heard of at a Theosophical Society meeting. There, according to Griff, his mother had been brainwashed by a fake guru. And then something bad had happened to her, and she had ended up in the asylum.

As soon as she started singing with Griff and Marty, Lizbie became aware of the young women who circled them, looking for a way in. Few found it. The two were immersed in music, and it was Lizbie's luck that she could sing. She'd passed grade six piano, too, and they got her a keyboard, and worked out some arrangements. The three of them gigged in all kinds of venues, from bars to private parties, occasionally getting in a drummer to beef up the sound, and bringing out the electric guitar and bass. The longer they made music together the more deeply Lizbie became embedded in their lives, although as Marty told her once when he was stoned – he would always be closer to Griff than to anyone: Lizbie should have taken it as a warning, but she'd been stoned herself.

She had lied to the shrink about sleeping with Marty. They had tried often enough, always because Lizbie had willed it, because she had got them to a place where it could happen, but they had never fully succeeded. This thwarting only fanned Lizbie's desire. She was consumed with a scorching, helpless love for Marty, that at least she knew enough not to declare.

One afternoon, after a worse than usual argument with her mother, Lizbie had found herself homeless, and Marty had asked his mother if she could stay at *Winterbourne* until she got her own place. To Lizbie's joy, Claire had acquiesced. Marty had helped lug Lizbie's belongings up to the attic room next to his own, and crashed on the bed to watch her unpack.

"You're sure your folks don't mind me staying?"

Marty's smile was wry. "Mum's convinced you're going to make a man of me."

Lizbie had paused with her arms full of crumpled clothes and looked at Marty – his secretive eyes and his evasive mouth, the shadows in his face that gave him a suffering, patient look: he could have played Jesus Christ and never had to work at the part, she thought. And she had chosen not to understand, because if she were being honest, Lizbie had already guessed that Marty was gay. It was just that somehow – and perhaps his mother felt the same – she hoped it wouldn't be permanent.

Marty was in his second year of architecture, and beginning to realise it wasn't what he wanted to do; Griff had dropped out of med school after a year and was working in a surf shop; Lizbie was waitressing in a vegetarian restaurant. They hung out together at a wine bar called Moby Dick's. It was on one of the beachside strips not far from where Griff lived. The owner, Raymond, gave them regular Sunday afternoon gigs. He was the first guy Lizbie had ever met who was openly camp. Most nights, Moby Dick's was full of young men. There would always be stray girls, like Lizbie, who were somehow attached to them, and a few of those were what Raymond mockingly referred to as 'beards'. If she'd ever had any doubts about Marty they fell away at Moby Dick's, for it was impossible not to notice how his body took on a new, more languid set of gestures in Raymond's presence; even the way he turned his head was different.

Lizbie, inwardly squirming, suspected that Marty had slept with Raymond, and she wondered whether, behind her back, Raymond referred to her as a 'beard'. Meanwhile, Griff was his usual laid-back surfer-boy self; he was amiable towards Raymond, and around him and his friends his body language never altered.

On the third or fourth Sunday gig at Moby Dick's, Lizbie realised in a flash of insight that her love for Marty had withered. Loving him was a one-way transaction; it had become untenable. It was then that she had turned to Griff.

Despite herself, she goes back to the shrink. Perhaps she has become addicted to sitting in an ugly chair and trawling through the past; or perhaps, after all, there is comfort in talking, rather than cycling through these events over and over in her head, allowing them to herd her towards her own madness.

"Griff had his hang-ups," she says. "His mother going off when he was young had screwed him over, but in every other respect he was straightforward, compared to Marty."

"So Marty was gay, and Griff was straight?"

"Before I met them, Griff would swing either way." Lizbie sighs, and is silent.

Eventually, the woman prompts her. "Their partnership had been sexual as well as musical, until you joined them."

Lizbie rakes a hand through her hair. "Yeah, I guess."

"You guess, or you know?"

She nods, resigned to where the conversation must go. "In high school they used to get stoned together, and experiment sexually," she said. "But Marty had been with other boys; he always had lovers, whereas Griff only ever had Marty."

"Then Griff fell in love with you."

"I think he was just waiting for me to realise I was never going to get anywhere with Marty. That happened around the time that Griff's father died, and I moved into their house out at the beach," she says. "The place was a wreck, because Griff's dad never had another relationship after his wife left, so you can imagine, three men living on their own for years, nobody keeping things straight."

The shrink nods, and makes a note in her file.

"That's when Marty progressed from smoking dope to using," says Lizbie. "He got into it with a few people he'd met at Moby Dick's. I don't know, maybe Raymond was a dealer."

"Was it because you had come between Marty and Griff?"

"Well, yeah, and the fact that the music scene had changed out of all recognition. Who would want to dance to someone playing records? That's what we thought when we first heard about disco, but when it took off, live music was ruined. For years there we were only playing sporadically. Raymond still gave us gigs; there were still private parties, but not like before."

The shrink scribbles something else in her file, and Lizbie wonders what it can be.

"Griff and I were happy," she says. "We had the sweetest wedding. In his white suit he was so beautiful he could have been the bride, and I was in a second-hand white dress with a little wreath of roses on my head; Griff said I looked like Ophelia. There were no bridesmaids, no best man. Maybe Griff didn't want to ask Marty. We just walked into the place together, and walked out as man and wife." She pauses, takes a sip from the glass of water beside her. "I guess we were playing at being grownups all through the early eighties. Griff had started talking about going back to study part time. He knew he didn't have the stomach for medicine, but something else. I thought he'd have made a great teacher – he was always so calm and patient; he saw the good in everyone."

Lizbie sits in silence, allowing the grief that rises in her to settle. As she has been taught to do by an earlier therapist, she visualises breathing it out into the room like smoke, letting it drift out the window and away over the rooftops.

"After you were married, did you see much of Marty, outside of the gigs?"

"All the time. We never fell out, although it sometimes got a bit strained between them. Marty would come out to the house a couple of times a week, and I'd make a curry with vegetables I'd grown in the garden, or I'd do lasagne because they both adored it. We'd eat, and then smoke, and sit around the kitchen playing music just for the pleasure of it. Those nights were some of the happiest of my life," she says.

"What caused strain between them?" asks the therapist.

"Oh, Marty's drug use. Griff worried about him. And Marty would laugh at us, poke fun. He would say that next thing we'd be decorating a nursery – he had a genuine horror of babies and pregnant women. It used to rile Griff, because we had talked about having kids one day."

"And Marty's overdose was accidental?"

They are moving out into the deep water now. Suddenly Lizbie is willing the clock to complete the hour and free her from the chair.

"I think it was, even though people said he'd been depressed."

"But not so low he would have ended his life?"

"Music was still doing it for Marty. He was writing songs, and planning to record; he had booked a studio and asked Griff to play flute and bass." Lizbie leans forward in the chair as if rejecting its padded comfort. "But there were other places he'd go to – clubs where you had to know someone to get in. When Marty got beaten up outside one of them he had to tell his parents he'd been mugged somewhere else." She chews her lip, and subsides into the chair.

"So Marty's parents didn't know he was gay?"

"I'd say his mother suspected. But they were the straightest people on the planet, he could never have told them." Lizbie shrugs. "And then their marriage was in trouble. So yeah, I guess things had begun to pile up for Marty. But I still think he would have left a note. He'd have wanted to dramatize the moment."

Perhaps the clock has stopped. Lizbie wants to leap up and out the door, but there is no escape.

"And what was it like in the aftermath?"

How to describe those freefalling days after Marty died, with Griff refusing to get out of bed, to wash, or eat. Unable to comfort him, Lizbie had sat at the kitchen table and considered setting fire to the house; she'd called Lifeline and talked to someone for two and a half hours; she had walked to the beach and considered throwing herself off the jetty, just so she wouldn't have to go back and witness the extent of her husband's grief. Would Griff have been this way if she had died? It was hard to imagine. He loved her, she was certain, but it looked like he'd loved Marty more. She'd been so confused, so lost; she hadn't known where to turn. In the end she'd gone back and crawled in beside him, and after a while the two of them had pulled themselves up out of the nose dive, more or less.

"Yeah, it was full on with Griff."

"And how long afterwards was it that he got the diagnosis?"

A year had dragged by that had seemed like a decade. Then Griff had started forcing himself to do things again.

"It was a year and three months after Marty died."

"How did he find out?"

"Oh, ever since med school Griff had been a blood donor; he was one of the rare types, so he went once or twice a year to give blood. This time they were running low, so the blood bank had called."

"And his donation screened positive for HIV."

"Apparently. He never had that conversation with me, he just …"

Again she has to wait while the feelings pass through her, only this time it takes so long that the therapist rises.

"I'm so sorry, Lizbie, that we have to end at this point. If you were able to wait until my next client leaves we could ..."

Lizbie stands up. "No, it's okay. Well, not okay, but obviously I've talked about this before."

The woman opens the door for her, and Lizbie passes out into the reception area; it is filled with people waiting to see other shrinks, to see her shrink, people who don't look as if their worlds are ending. She books an appointment for the following week, but in her mind she's already calling to cancel.

Lizbie has been screened, and it has come back negative. But down the track there will be further screenings, and this is what everyone assumes she is most disturbed by. But everything disturbs her; any small thing is likely to tip her over the edge. Like that phone call from Claire Delaney when she and her husband were getting divorced and Claire wanted to know whether Lizbie would take their cat. Holding the phone, with Claire's voice in her ear, she had nearly screamed: "No! I can't look after anything, not even myself." But then she'd recalled how when she had been homeless Claire had given her shelter.

She wonders whether Claire even knew Marty was HIV positive. Well whatever: Lizbie wasn't going to tell her. But the thing she can't get out of her head, the thing that bedevils her days, is that while she was cooking curries, while she was pottering among her tomato plants and lettuces like Sunbonnet Sue, Marty and Griff had been lovers. They had been lovers while Griff was whispering to her in bed at night about one day raising a family, while they were picking out their favourite names. Griff had sworn to her he was done with all that; she had strengthened his heterosexual side, he said, and that was how it was going to stay. But Marty had taken Griff back from her, and she hadn't even known: her glory days had been fewer than she'd thought.

Lizbie thinks of the two of them as she saw them first – they had been so beautiful that it had hurt to look at them for long. But their beauty hadn't lasted, not for Marty with his ugly heroin death, not for Griff, who had found his dad's old shotgun and taken it out to the back shed. Lizbie nurtures Claire's cat that for years slept on Marty's pillow. She goes to, or doesn't go to, various appointments; she struggles to keep the house tidy while she waits to hear whether she is in the clear. And sometimes on a Sunday morning she takes the bus across town and walks past the old house where *Winterbourne* is written in faded black letters on the gate. The cypress hedge is no longer sharp; large sections of it are dying. Lizbie lingers in its shade as she listens for Marty's artless guitar playing, for their two voices, with her own voice between. And it strikes her that there should have been a way for the three of them to express their love, some form of marriage that didn't depend on one of them being excluded.

Walking away, she hears her mother complain that this is what comes of wearing a see-through blouse. But Lizbie knows it is what comes with the shifts and swings of people's lives, the swerving patterns you can never see. And it is, too, what comes when dumb fate leads you to turn right into a certain street on a certain morning, when you might as easily have turned left, or when you might have listened, and then walked away without applauding.

The Lives We Lost

The rooms Jeanie sleeps in now are all the same – crammed with the excess baggage of people's lives, the belongings they can't bring themselves to cull, and the remains of childhoods, abruptly abandoned. She never lets on how the clutter, with its sifting of dust, presses around her in the dark. Jeanie is grateful for a bed, and for the reticence of people who would rather she moved on.

The latest room is as cluttered and ugly as its predecessors. The second bedroom in a second-floor, two-bedroom flat; its window overlooks a side fence and a busy bus stop. The curtains, a dull rust that might have once been red, have shrunk in some long ago spring-cleaning wash so that they no longer touch the sill. At night, the exposing width of darkened glass troubles Jeanie more than the towers of plastic storage boxes. Before dressing or undressing she fills the gap with two rolled-up bath towels.

The flat belongs to a cousin she has scarcely seen since primary school. Sue Hawe is the daughter of Jeanie's mother's youngest brother. A rift between their families, which neither of them can remember or explain, means they share a few vivid early memories, and then nothing, until Jeanie called and asked if Sue could put her up.

"Oh, sure! I'd love to see you," Sue said. "So what, a couple of days? A week?"

Jeanie has slept in Sue's spare room for almost three months, to her host's mounting antagonism.

Until her thirty-fifth year, Jeanie's life had followed its expected curve, from childhood to marriage and motherhood, with a few years in between as a dental hygienist. At her wedding to Rob Tarrant, luminous in a pearl-white guipure lace gown, exhilarated beneath a mist of veil, Jeanie had felt an almost holy sense of purpose. Her life's trajectory had been clear: she'd had no doubts. That certainty would last until their second child Madeleine was about to start school. By then Jeanie and Rob had settled into their house on the new estate, which when the gardens and street trees matured, would be as enviably leafy as the suburb where Jeanie had been raised. Their son and daughter had both been born healthy; they were bright. Jeanie had believed her cup of happiness was full.

And then in bed one night in the thin summer darkness, at a moment of unguarded emotion that owed something to a long, boozy dinner with friends, Rob blurted out that he hadn't been in love on their wedding day.

"But I love you now, Jeanie," he moaned. "I love you so much."

Pressed into the mattress, Jeanie had become deathly still. Could what Rob had said be true? All these years, wouldn't she have known if he had been pretending?

"What do you mean?" she breathed into his ear, softly, dangerously.

Rob peeled damply away from her and rolled onto his back. "I'm saying I love you," he said. "That's all."

"What about when we were married?" she persisted.

In the dark he found her hand and squeezed it. "Well, I had always planned to settle down by the time I was twenty-eight. It felt like the right age, you know, to have kids. There was never anyone special, but you were the steadiest girl I knew; I was sure you'd make a good wife and mother. So after the courting, I proposed. I always knew in my head that it was right, but I had never felt it in my heart, until now."

"What, you mean until tonight?"

"Not tonight – just lately. This past year. It's been growing on me."

Lying on her back in the stuffy bedroom, sticky with sweat and semen, Jeanie had said quietly, "I see."

She wondered about this steadiness Rob had detected in her, and valued. It was true that she had not been as flighty as some of her teenage friends, had never gone in for hysterics, or fits of the giggles, or for acting out and upsetting her parents. She'd always had her homework done; her grades were good, though she was never top of the class. Jeanie had been a house captain, and a prefect. A dentist's daughter, her teeth had been naturally straight without the need for bands. She was good-looking rather than pretty, which was much the best, her mother assured her, because good looks last.

In her final year of high school Jeanie had almost swerved off course. She'd had a serious crush on her art teacher, Mr Deverill. His dark hair curled over his collar; he rarely wore a tie, and somehow got away with this departure from school etiquette. Jeanie had once seen him coming out of a picture theatre wearing tight black jeans and a leather jacket, looking immensely cool. Mr Deverill had read into Jeanie's constant presence a budding passion for art. He'd introduced her to Matisse and Bonnard, his personal favourites, and Jeanie made up her mind to go to art school. Her imagination had seized on the romance of the artistic life, and she pictured herself in a studio with high, uncurtained windows, wearing a paint-stained smock like Berthe Morisot, or Mary Cassatt.

"Artists are born with all the resources they need inside them," Mr Deverill said. "They create out of their own personal light."

Jeanie had felt a tremor of sadness for Mr Deverill, that his inner light had been dimmed, or even extinguished, by the need to teach. She had felt her own light shining clear and strong. But her mother had sat with her all one long summer afternoon and patiently pointed out that art school would take her far from home. There was no certainty in the artistic life, whereas she could study right here to become a dental assistant; she could gain work experience in her father's practice. When she married and had children she would always be able to find paid, part-time employment, whereas as an artist, who knew if she would ever earn anything? Resistant at first, Jeanie had at last caved in to parental pressure. But there were times, staring over the edge of her mask at a bleeding gum, when she had wanted to hurl the probe or the suction tube across the room.

In the aftermath of Rob's revelation there was no noticeable change in their lives, but below the surface tectonic plates were shifting. Jeanie bought a box of watercolour paints and a selection of sable brushes; she bought sheets of Arches paper, and a French watercolour easel. They were expensive, especially the easel and the numbers 12 and 14 sable brushes. Jeanie had worked part-time after Ben was born but then quit after Madeleine. The money for the art materials came from their joint account, but Jeanie wrote the cheque with a steady hand, as she would not have done even six months earlier.

When Maddy started school, instead of going back to work, Jeanie bought a second-hand bicycle. In the mornings, as soon as Rob left and she had walked the children to school, she packed her painting equipment and cycled away from the house, away from the suburbs.

The first time she approached Bailey's Wood Jeanie had burst out laughing: she was wearing a bright red jacket with a little hood. A council information board informed her that she was entering one of the few remaining semi-natural ancient woodlands, the habitat of various butterfly species, of birds such as the greater spotted woodpecker, the tree-creeper, and the nuthatch. The access tracks were in fair condition, though there were places where Jeanie had to dismount and haul the bike over rocks, or broken ground, or the roots of trees. If the wind was in a certain direction there was the distant roar of the motorway, but otherwise it was quiet. Bailey's Wood was a cool, green, private, and largely silent world, a place of dappled light and dissolving shadows that Jeanie felt had been waiting for her.

She went to the wood to paint nearly every weekday, packing a sandwich and staying until it was time to ride back and meet the children. When autumn came she went whenever the weather was dry, for rain muddied the paths and made cycling, or even walking, difficult. When she was unable to sketch and paint out of doors Jeanie felt listless and agitated; in the end she bought waterproofs and braved the weather.

When Jeanie first met Julian Holt she had been working her way around the western edge of the wood, avoiding the mud stirred by recent rains. He was walking ahead of her along a track between clumps of faded bracken, a lean old man, she first thought, and she would later learn that he would soon turn sixty. He walked with a slight stoop, as if he were searching for something. She watched him stop to catch his breath, and when they became friends he would explain that he was allergic to some of the plants he collected, that there were one or two that affected his breathing. When he heard her bicycle bell, he turned – eyes bright and inquisitive, mouth a generous curve under a close-cut beard; his once-dark hair was liberally streaked with grey, but it was still plentiful. He made room for her to pass, but it was impossible not to stop and speak to him, though Jeanie couldn't have said why.

She dismounted, and as they fell into conversation Jeanie caught herself thinking that Mr Deverill might look like this now, that they must be of a similar age. Julian showed her the different mosses he'd gathered in the hessian bag he carried.

"I've painted all of these," she said, "but I don't know their names."

So he laid the mosses across his palm one by one, and told her their Latin and common names: as with most plants, the common names were the most beautiful.

"Swan's-neck thyme moss, glittering wood moss, common haircap …"

Julian was writing a research paper on the historical uses of moss, everything from thatching and insulating houses to bandaging wounds. As they walked on together, he asked Jeanie about her painting.

The path they were following led to a lane, and eventually to a small wooden gate. Julian pointed to a squat stone hut – two windows, a red front door, a pitched slate roof topped by a chimney. All that was missing was a curl of smoke. This was where he was living while he completed his research.

"My daughter draws houses that look like this," Jeanie said.

After that she would skirt the wood, hoping to bump into him. Often she did, for in the mornings Julian wrote, and after lunch he went foraging. Once, when a heavy rain caught them in the open, he invited Jeanie to shelter in the cottage. Inside, the brick-floored main room had been arranged around an open fireplace; wire baskets of drying mosses hung from the beams, and there were worn Persian rugs to soften the bricks. A scrubbed pine dining table and two comfortable chairs drawn up beside the hearth, a divan that doubled as a couch, were the only furniture. To Jeanie's eyes, the bare, whitewashed walls were not stark, but serene.

In its simplicity, its confident use of natural materials, the woodcutter's cottage, for that was what it had once been, Julian said, could not have been more different to Jeanie's and Rob's house. Crouching in front of the fire in her scarlet jacket, Jeanie wanted to rush home and strip away all the bric-a-brac and knickknacks that cluttered their rooms; she thought with a surge of resentment that if she had held out for art school she might, by now, have been capable of designing an interior like this one.

Jeanie's woodland watercolours and drawings were delicate, Julian said, they were enchanting. He encouraged her to have them framed.

"You must put them where they can be seen."

Bolstered by his approval, Jeanie ordered double mounts, acid-free board, conservation glass. She stripped their house of ornaments, and when her first pictures came back from the framer she hung them on the walls. Rob had never complained when she bought art materials, though he sucked in a long breath when he saw the framer's bill. But he lamented loudly the disappearance of the china dogs and shepherdesses that had been bequeathed to them by his mother; he was infuriated by the sudden absence of his collection of beer steins and football memorabilia, and he demanded that all of it be returned, likewise the souvenirs of family holidays. Jeanie did not restore a single ornament; in fact she could not, for she had delivered them to a charity store.

When Rob said, "Well, I don't know whether I want to live in a bloody art gallery," Jeanie heard in her husband's voice a new belligerence.

That night, when he ran a hand along her hip as she lay curled away from him, Jeanie pretended to be asleep.

To Jeanie, the tone of their marriage had altered; it was taking place now in a different register. Yet they carried on as before, entertaining other couples most weekends, or being entertained. At one of these gatherings Jeanie emerged from her kitchen balancing a tray of drinks, to hear Barry Darkley mutter to Erris Cleary's husband that he supposed her paintings were a pretty good effort, but they didn't cut the mustard as Art. The two men were standing in front of the most recent of Jeanie's woodland studies. Sensing her approach, they had turned towards her and raised their glasses. Barry's smile was a little embarrassed: he must have suspected that she had overheard.

Jeanie did not allow what Barry had said to fully sink in, not then and there. And this would be the way she would always deal with rejection and criticism: she would put it aside to examine later, in private, when there was no one to see if she cried. Barry Darkley couldn't have known that his casual remark would touch Jeanie's rawest nerve, the one that feared the work she cared about was simply self-taught illustration, that in spite of Julian's cautious praise it was mediocre.

Winter light is the most beautiful of all – silvery, pure, vacillating. In the wood, hunched over her easel and shivering a little inside her coat, Jeanie would look up into a slant of cloud-filtered light and long to stand naked under its piercing shower. If clarity was a reward for the season's austerity, poor weather meant there were days at a time when she was unable to ride to the wood. Either it rained steadily, there were gales, or it threatened to snow. Trapped at home, she thought of Julian, snug in his cottage, a wisp of smoke rising from the chimney. Soon he would finish writing up his research and leave. One day she would pedal up the lane and find the cottage empty.

Since the first time she sheltered there from the rain, Jeanie had often sat by Julian's fire. They had been drinking hot chocolate together when he had asked about her children. She had talked about Ben and Maddie, and how sometimes she looked at them as they slept and wondered how she could have produced such perfect little creatures. Julian had busied himself with the fire, but before he turned away Jeanie had read in his eyes that he thought she was beautiful, and that naturally her children would be beautiful, too, and this flash of naked admiration warmed her. Rob had never looked at her in that way, not even now, when he claimed to finally be in love.

Julian's wife was named Diana. They had been married for more than thirty years.

"Ovarian cancer put an end to the dream of children," he said. "Diana survived the cancer but not the childlessness." Julian's voice was heavy. "She changed so much," he said. "It was like being married to a different person."

"I'm so sorry," Jeanie said, instantly regretting having boasted of the perfection of her children. "I was one of the lucky ones."

Julian shrugged. "Diana was hospitalised with an eating disorder. It comes and goes even now. She may never be cured."

"You stuck together through all of that," Jeanie said.

"We did, though we are each in our own ways quite solitary."

It was why he could spend three months collecting mosses, and writing. Diana, too, spent long periods away from home. Currently, she was in Ethiopia. Julian had catalogued mosses on Dartmoor, and on the Burren. Jeanie learned that he had written a history of the moss gatherers of Dartmoor in the First World War, and of the moss factory, privately financed by the Prince of Wales, that had turned sphagnum moss into wound dressings for the Red Cross.

"They were cranked into service again during the Second World War," he told her.

The more time Jeanie spent with Julian, the harder it was to be with Rob. What did they ever talk about, other than the children? Entering a room, Rob's once reassuring bulk now seemed to absorb most of the oxygen, most of the light. Yet Jeanie recognised that her husband was the same as he had always been – it was she who was different. Just how different, she could not have articulated, but if pushed she would have said that the disenchantment with her marriage had begun with Rob's confession that he had not been in love with her on their wedding day. That knowledge had ignited a slow-burning resentment, a feeling that she had been taken in, acquired as a brood mare, not valued for who she was. If she had known at the time, it might have been grounds for an annulment.

Jeanie saw herself floating up the aisle, sacrificial under the mist of her veil. As she had stood beside Rob at the altar she had felt as if the two of them were lifted up together into a high place, 'a sacred mountain', she had said to herself at the time. Now she saw that she had been as alone on the mountain as under the veil, and she felt a vengeful desire to punish Rob.

Once it becomes clear that you are not a guest but something less transitory, camping in someone else's home is like the Chinese water torture. Drip drip drip. Jeanie and Sue have exhausted the conversations about places and people they knew as children. Drip drip drip. Jeanie has emptied her sympathy over Sue's acrimonious divorce, and the rejecting behaviour of her ungrateful children. Sue has listened to Jeanie explain how a life that once seemed so solid has mysteriously evaporated.

Neither cousin understands what the other is saying. Though they speak the same language, words, sentences, turn opaque when they attempt to describe their lives. Jeanie strains to imagine Sue's ex-husband impregnating the eighteen-year-old daughter of a couple he and Sue have known and socialised with since they were first married; she tries to see it as a lapse of judgement, or as a straight betrayal, but in the end all she sees is the abuse of a young and emotionally fragile young woman by a man Jeanie recalls unflatteringly as flashy, superficially attractive, a predatory alpha male. Understandably, the children want nothing to do with their father. Meanwhile, Sue purses her lips over Jeanie's artistic ambition.

"How could you give up your home, your family, over wall art?" Her face is a study of incomprehension and dismay.

Jeanie shrugs. "I know it must seem strange."

But Sue isn't listening. Drip drip drip. She asks whether Jeanie can pitch in some cash for the weekly food shop.

Julian had begun to appear uneasy when Jeanie came to the cottage. She wondered whether he was preparing to leave, and couldn't bring herself to ask. What she craved was more time in the wood, longer conversation with Julian, so she arranged for a child minder to pick up Ben and Maddy from school on Wednesday afternoons. Of course it all depended on the weather, and there would be days of pelting rain when leaving home was not even an option. So the arrangement was kept fluid: Jeanie would ring the child minder on a Wednesday morning if she wanted her to collect Ben and Maddy.

The first two Wednesdays had been sunny, though cold. For the first time, there was no pressure to return before the home-time bell. On the third Tuesday, Rob went to a work mate's boozy farewell, and when he stumbled in close to midnight and climbed into bed beside her, Jeanie had felt the heat of his intention to have sex, and was repelled. Curled against her resisting back, he slipped an arm around her waist and pulled her close; his hand found the opening in the top of her nightdress and fumbled its way inside.

"Please, it's late." Jeanie feigned sleepiness.

He pinched her nipple. "Come on, it's not as late as all that."

She flinched and pulled away, but he had lifted the hem of her nightdress and slid his hand between her thighs.

Jeanie propelled herself up and off the bed, and flicked on the light. "I'm sorry," she said, "I'm not feeling that great."

Rob, his face flushed, hurled a pillow at her. "Frigid bitch!"

Jeanie switched off the light, and went next door to creep in beside Maddy. She feared Rob would follow and drag her back to bed, but he must have rolled over and fallen asleep.

In the morning, Jeanie's hands shook as she buttered toast, made coffee, filled bowls with cereal for the children. Rob left for work without speaking, and when Jeanie had walked the children to school she jumped on her bicycle and pedalled madly towards Bailey's Wood.

Stray snowflakes fluttered around her as she sped along the path to the cottage. In the milk-pale light the shapes of evergreens stood out, dark and sombre, alongside pockets of deciduous larch. She threw down the bicycle in the lane and knocked at the red door. When Julian opened it she gasped with relief, for there had been no smoke, and the place looked deserted.

"Am I interrupting?" she said. "I'm sorry ..."

He held the door open for her, his forehead creased with surprise. "I haven't got the fire going yet," he said. "But there's coffee."

The table was covered in his papers and notebooks. Beside one of the chairs, a stack of text books, an empty wine glass. Jeanie imagined him sitting beside the fire last night, reading, sipping wine, while she had been lying in bed listening for Rob to come home.

"I'll bring in some kindling," he said.

The room was filled with the blue-white light of the unshed snow. Through the window the flank of the wood reared up, ancient, implacable; it would exist when she and Julian and Rob, when all of them, even Maddy and Ben, were gone. All the way to the cottage the memory of Rob calling her frigid had filled her with a swelling rage, but his voice was muted now, her anger less urgent than her need to see again the expression she had once surprised on Julian's face. She could hear him outside snapping small branches as she peeled off her coat, as she bent to unlace her boots; she pulled her jumper and shirt over her head in one movement, and dropped them on the floor. When he appeared in the doorway, she was naked.

Slowly, Julian lowered the kindling onto the hearth. Jeanie didn't move as he crossed to her and laid his hand on her arm.

"Are you all right?" he said.

"Yes."

The expression she sought was there in his eyes – desire, tinged with reverence.

He brushed the blade of her collarbone with a fingertip. "My God," he said, "you really are a most beautiful woman."

Jeanie closed her eyes. She wanted to give freely to this man what she had withheld from Rob. She would have laid down on the rug with Julian, or on the divan that was still unmade from where he had slept.

She began to cry, and he put his arms around her. "You're cold," he said.

Jeanie shook her head. "No."

She felt his warmth against her breasts, against the small white mound of her belly. Now that she had started crying, Jeanie found she could not stop. Julian pulled the cover from the divan and wrapped it around her; he held her close, and they stood there beside the unlit fire for what felt like a long, long time.

Sue becomes beady-eyed when Jeanie says she can't contribute towards the electricity bill.

"But I'll have a cheque next week. I'll be able to make it up to you then."

Her cousin's lips are two thin lines.

"I don't know about next week," Sue says. "Look, it's time to speak plainly. I mean, we were related as kids, but I hardly know you now. You could be anyone."

On the Wednesday when it had threatened to snow, Jeanie went to the wood without calling the child minder. After school, Maddy and Ben waited at the school gates but there was no one to meet them or to see them home safe. It came to

Jeanie in a flood of horror that turned her limbs to water, as she cycled up the drive and saw Rob's car.

All their downstairs lights were blazing. In their kitchen, their neighbour with the too-tight perm and inquisitive eyes stood stirring scrambled eggs in a pan. Seated at the table, Maddy and Ben looked limp from crying. When Jeanie loomed in the doorway Rob glared, then jerked his head towards the study.

Jeanie describes the destruction of her marriage, but Sue does not see that it only takes the slightest shift in purpose to spin a life off course.

"You make a defensive turning, or you swerve towards some perceived excitement," Jeanie says.

Sue stares at her like she is crazy, and Jeanie makes up her mind to leave.

The cottage was empty when she went back. Afterwards, because of Ben and Maddy, she tried to re-enter her own life, but it was closed. Rob moved out. Eventually, the children grew up and left home. For a while Jeanie struggled to maintain the mortgage. Her parents developed dementia, and their house was sold to pay the nursing home. Rob married again, and he and his new wife had two more children. Maddy settled in London, Ben in Prague. Jeanie started to sleep in people's guest rooms.

"Once the curve of a life is altered it will never again be as it was, even though you throw your whole self into restoring it," says Jeanie.

Sue rolls her eyes. They are out of coffee; it's Jeanie's turn to walk to the shop.

"And when one life loses direction, those closest are nudged into new orbits; some constellations appear, and others vanish."

When Jeanie learned to use a computer, and the Internet, she found Julian's obituary. Julian Barrington Holt had died at sixty-five of pancreatic cancer; a notable bryologist and lichenologist, he was survived by his wife Diana.

When Jeanie's life lost its direction, those closest to her were thrown into new orbits. Since then she has watched countless lives soar and plunge amid trails of sparks and burning debris. Witnessing their destruction gives her no pleasure.

This Moment Is Your Life

Delia makes her first serious public slip at a family christening. The ceremony is held outdoors in a sunny garden, among old apple trees just coming into blossom and twenty or thirty rose bushes frantic with their first flush of blooms. The roses are yellow, red, and a coral shade Delia particularly dislikes. A few are even multi-coloured – yellow streaked with scarlet – altogether a cacophony of colour that grates on Delia's nerves. She is frowning over this, when a young woman walks towards her holding a baby in christening robes. The woman pauses in front of Delia and raises the sleeping infant a little higher to show them his face, for Malcolm is hovering at Delia's shoulder.

"He's sweet," Delia says, a frown puckering her forehead. "Where did you get him?"

The young woman's broad smile falters. "Well, he's *ours*," she says, "mine and Carl's. This is Theo!"

Malcolm's hand comes swiftly to rest in the small of Delia's back, as if to support her if she should topple. Theo? The name rings in her head, but it has a meaningless echo in connection with this young woman and her child. The girl's open, freckled face is familiar, but Delia cannot at that moment summon her name. Who is this person holding baby Theo, and staring at her with an almost terrified expression?

Malcolm glides to her rescue. "Pauline and Carl chose the name Theo for their son in memory of your father, Delia. You told me you were very touched that they'd done that."

"Oh, yes," she says gratefully. "Theo is a beautiful name."

And it really is a beautiful name, one Delia associates with patience, and tenderness, and old-fashioned courtesy. It's just that this Pauline, who has taken for her tiny son the name of Delia's father, is a mystery to her. They must be related, surely. Or why make a point about the name? But related in what way? When she poses the question her mind comes up blank.

"I'm so glad you approve." Pauline's smile has faded. She glances around the garden. "There are some seats under the apple trees," she says. "Would you like me to send Carl over with a drink?"

People are strolling past them with champagne flutes, and Delia thinks it might be pleasant to sit in the dappled light under the trees and fill her mouth with cold bubbles, to let them glide down her throat until the sense of calm and well-being alcohol always brings erases this moment of awkwardness and confusion.

"Two sparkling waters, please," Malcolm says. "We have a long drive to get home."

"Sure. I'll tell Carl."

Pauline backs away from them, while Delia stares into the golden curves of a rose, resentful at being denied champagne, grateful to Malcolm for covering for her.

Malcolm's voice is pitched so only Delia can hear, as he seeks to ease her confusion. "Your niece, Pauline, she's lovely."

Delia dares not speak, or even look at Malcolm.

Five years before the afternoon of Theo's christening, Delia and Malcolm were married. In the interval between those two events, Malcolm, a retired lecturer in structural engineering, has been designing, and then building, the eco-house where he and Delia now live. Constructed using materials and technology that reduces its carbon footprint, their corner house is surrounded on two sides by high gabion walls. Delia has learned that the word 'gabion' comes from the Italian *gabbione*, or 'big cage', and that Leonardo da Vinci designed a gabion for the foundations of the San Marco Castle in Milan.

"It was called a *corbeille Leonard*, or 'Leonardo basket'." Malcolm has never lost his zeal for teaching.

The small weatherboard house that had previously stood on the site had been surrounded by old fruit trees, and by carefully managed plantings of pale roses, and medicinal herbs, kept just tidy enough not to look untended. It must have belonged to a good witch, Delia thought the first time she saw it; a wise woman who would have turned the herbs into healing salves, into life-saving remedies, perhaps even into love potions. Malcolm had stamped up and down the brick-paved paths, crushing violets, and lady's mantle growing between the cracks. He pointed out to Delia the building's lack of insulation, its woeful plumbing, the water-hungry orange and lemons trees.

"But we can keep the peach trees, surely," Delia said. "Peaches and quinces thrive in a Mediterranean climate."

Malcolm shook his head. "They'll look out of place alongside succulents and natives."

So the block was ruthlessly cleared, and slowly Malcolm's dream house emerged out of the raw scraped soil, a house with an air of being barricaded against attack, plain-faced behind its gabion walls. Malcolm explained to passers-by who had stopped to watch the fencers at work that the life expectancy of gabions relies on the lifespan of the wire, not on the contents of the basket.

"The structure will fail when the wire fails," he said.

At the end, a team of landscape gardeners had moved in and planted tough native shrubs and wild grasses to Malcolm's design. In time these developed messy growth habits, until Delia had trouble telling which were the plants and which were weeds. The wire cages packed with rocks, too, were something of an eyesore. She felt like apologising to their neighbours, and to the woman with the picket fence across the street whose front windows faced their gabion wall, with its stepped-back pockets of spiky, weed-like grasses. But Malcolm was so clearly pleased with the whole effect, and Delia, who was secretly a little frightened by the relentless creep of her memory loss, kept her opinions to herself.

A couple of years before Delia and Malcolm married, they had abandoned their separate living arrangements – a run-down but convivial share house for Delia, and a one-bedroom flat close to the university for Malcolm – and moved into a two-storey town house Malcolm had inherited from his mother: it was the eventual sale of this place that would finance their eco-house. Delia was both excited and nervous at the commitment this move implied. It wasn't that she didn't love Malcolm, but she had been so long on her own, and while she had shared domestic spaces with other people it had always felt somewhat temporary; housemates came and went as their circumstances changed, so that Delia could have moved on at any time without tears or ill feeling.

Moving in with Malcolm was different. Delia found herself thinking back to the misery of living with, and leaving, her first husband, of how Roger had cowed her, physically and mentally, until she had agreed to let him take Josh and be satisfied with keeping Katie. If she forced him to go to court he would take both children, Roger had said. Delia had believed him, for although her husband had failed his law exams and gone into insurance, his father was a senior partner in a law firm. The court would hear of her depraved behaviour, Roger threatened. Delia had no idea what he meant, but she had known when she was beaten.

Women in Roger's family did not go out to work, and after their honeymoon Roger had suggested that Delia quit her job. She was receptionist to an accountant and the work was dull, so she hadn't minded; once they had children she wouldn't be able to, anyway. But then when she'd wanted to leave Roger, she saw the trap. With no money, beyond what little she could borrow from friends, Delia had signed the papers her husband had drawn up, and watched him drive off with Josh's face a pale blur in the car's rear window. It was years before she saw her son again, and when she did he was angry with her. By then Delia had concluded that those papers Rob had pressed her to sign might not have held up in a court, that most likely he had been bluffing, but it was too late for her and Josh.

While she was packing to move into Malcolm's place, Delia considered keeping her books in storage for a while, in case things didn't work out. There were boxes and boxes of them, the spoils of having worked in a bookshop for almost twenty years, too many to shift by herself. Aside from the books, she lived lightly, and could have packed up and moved all her belongings in the boot of her small hatchback. But even to be thinking this way seemed half-hearted, a betrayal; it was tempting fate to bring her relationship with Malcolm crashing down at the first hurdle. How could they form a lasting partnership if she wasn't prepared to bring her whole self to it? Hadn't this always been her trouble?

When she dithered for too long over the move, Malcolm had come and helped her pack. Delia took the books. Eventually, when she'd seemed reluctant to deal with the boxes of belongings piled up in the garage at the townhouse, he had helped her to open them, and that was how he came upon the shoe box full of old photographs.

Delia had forgotten its existence, but the moment she saw it in Malcolm's hands she felt a rush of recognition, a twist of anxiety in her gut. Once he'd realised what the box contained, Malcolm was jubilant.

"At last," he said, "a clue as to who this woman I'm planning on spending the rest of my life with really is!"

Delia had smiled weakly, wondering what was in the box, hoping she'd disposed of anything that would make her feel tacky or ridiculous. There were times when she, too, would have welcomed a clue to who she was, and who she had once been, though she didn't fancy receiving these revelations in Malcolm's presence.

Together they inspected snapshots of a younger Delia pushing Katie on a swing, feeding ducks on a pond, blowing out three candles on a cake for Josh, whose solemn little face looked so much like Delia's. There was a photograph of Delia and Roger and the children standing in the driveway of the last house they had lived in together. That suburb where the smell of barbequed meat hung in the air on fine weekends, and where the magpies had sung in the early mornings as Delia stumbled from bed after a night of broken sleep, to change nappies, to set out the breakfast dishes, to make coffee for Roger before he left for work.

"What's going on in this one?"

Malcolm passed it to Delia, a Polaroid photograph, milky with age. It showed a brick-paved suburban patio at night; adults in fancy dress, drinking and dancing. They had been partying for some time judging by the sweaty faces of the drinkers, the abandon of the dancers.

Delia held the picture gingerly by its white borders and peered into it, at first with a look of wonder and then with a secretive narrowing of her eyes. There she was, flame-haired, with a high, choppy fringe that exposed her eyebrows, red-lipstick mouth caught half open, like the mouth of a goldfish, or a porn star. What astonished her was her own raw beauty; at the time, she had judged herself awkward looking, even plain. She had sewn the flapper dress herself out of a pair of old lace curtains. To her relief the figure she was dancing with was a blur, except for one pinstriped sleeve and an inch of white shirt-cuff.

"Who's this?" Over Delia's shoulder, Malcolm pointed to her dance partner.

Delia shrugged. "No idea. Just someone who was at the party, I guess."

It was Erris Cleary, her savage haircut plastered to her skull with her husband's Brylcreem, Erris as Jay Gatsby in an op-shop suit. Among a group of men standing to one side of the dancers, Roger's face was swollen with drink and disgust. Malcolm didn't notice this, so Delia said nothing. Erris's husband, the doctor, was nowhere in sight, having stalked off to retrieve their coats just before the picture was taken. Delia recalled the flash-bulb exploding, and how moments later he had loomed beside them, long thin fingers clamped around Erris's wrist.

"Time to go," he said. "You've had too much to drink."

Without breaking step, Erris had twisted free. "But I'm having so much fun," she said. "And I'm not ready to leave."

That morning, Delia and Erris had gone together to the hairdresser, both, as they discovered on the bus, disgusted with their husbands – Erris because she had learned that John Cleary had talked to her gynaecologist about her at a hospital social function, Delia because Roger refused to eat cereal and insisted she cook bacon and eggs, even on mornings when she'd been up and down all night to the children. Delia hadn't known that Erris was planning such a radical cut, and she'd been shocked to see her hair lying on the floor of the salon – a warm chestnut mass, enough to stuff a small pillow. Meanwhile, another stylist had talked Delia into a new kind of perm. She called it a 'Min Vague', and afterwards Delia's hair was minimally curly, it was vaguely waved: the two of them had almost wet themselves laughing at this as they walked from the salon. At the bus stop, helpless with laughter, they had waved the first bus on and waited for the next one.

It was Erris's haircut that had shocked people as much as anything she did that night. After all, everyone was drinking, everyone was dancing, just not as wildly as Erris, and not with just one partner. But it was as if the hilarity of the morning had crept into their bones; they felt awfully *avant-garde* in their retro dress-ups, they felt, as they screamed to each other over the music, "so Min Vague!"

Delia didn't remember getting home from that party, but she remembered Roger dismissing the babysitter and then dragging her into their bedroom. The flapper dress was curtains again; he pushed her down onto their bed.

"Roger, please! You'll wake the chil …"

Next day, as she nursed her hangover, Delia's right eye-socket had filled with blood. She had hidden it behind dark glasses, but everyone knew, from the teachers at Katie's school to the woman at the corner shop. For Delia, being punched by her husband marked the end of the marriage, though it had gone on a little longer while she worked out an escape plan. The strangest part was that she had not felt sexually attracted to Erris that night, as Roger had insisted everyone at the party believed. But in the weeks that followed, all she yearned for was to rest her cheek in the curve of Erris's white neck. She had imagined the two of them, lying together in a quiet, sunny bedroom, their soft exchange of breath, their bubbling laughter.

She had moved back to live with her mother. With Katie to care for, no job and no money, she'd had no choice. The first night after she left Roger, waking early, Delia had sat up and leaned into the lemon sunlight streaming through the uncurtained window, and the ache in her chest was all for Erris.

Delia's GP has carried out a cognitive assessment and the results are not as terrible as she has feared. Still, he recommends further tests with a memory specialist, and Malcolm takes her to the hospital for her appointment. They arrive with thirty minutes to spare, and slip into the ground floor cafe. The first person Delia sees is Claire Delaney – Claire, at whose house, all those years ago, the now infamous fancy dress party was held.

"Delia!"

Claire hasn't weathered too badly, considering the years that have passed.

"I'm waiting to visit a friend," Claire says. "It's Tommy's wife, Rosanna, actually."

Delia hears the words 'breast cancer', she hears 'double mastectomy'. She says how sorry she is. "It must be horrible." She asks Claire where she's living now, hoping she won't ask why she's at the hospital.

"I've been in the same little flat for years," Claire says.

Malcolm has drifted to the counter to order their coffee, so Delia tells Claire that she, too, would like somewhere smaller, but Malcolm is attached to their eco-house. While Claire describes where Tommy and Rosanna live, Delia allows herself to picture a cottage like the one their eco-house replaced, something pretty, with a soft brush fence rather than their rock-filled wire cage. The wire is beginning to show signs of wear, and this makes Delia anxious. She remembers Malcolm telling anyone who would listen that the life expectancy of gabions relies on the lifespan of the wire, not on the contents of the basket.

Delia flicks a nervous glance to where her husband hovers before a display of cakes, all of which are disastrous for his heart. He will not buy one for himself, but he will choose a treat for her, and as Claire rattles on about her ex-husband, Delia experiences a wave of affection for Malcolm. Ever since he stumbled into the bookshop that time, he has been doggedly devoted. She sees how dear he is, how gentle.

Claire is talking about Erris Cleary. "It was in the paper," she says. "She'd had a breakdown, but that was a while back."

"Oh! I had no idea."

Delia realises that Claire is speaking of Erris in the past tense, a mock-solemn tone that means Erris is dead, or in serious trouble. Delia tries to think … Erris had been the youngest of all of them … she can't be more than … fifty-two or three. With shocking clarity, Delia hears Erris's warm, cigarette-grained voice: *I was a child bride!* She hears her friend's self-deprecating laughter.

"There were a few from the old days at the funeral." Claire leans closer. "Not that she particularly cared for any of them."

Delia's throat aches with tears. Most days, she will struggle to remember what she ate for breakfast, yet suddenly here she is, flooded with grief for the loss of a long-ago moment, and for other moments that must have passed unnoticed between her and Erris – at all those barbecues in someone's garden, at the beach, or at drinks after tennis – moments around which her life might have begun to pivot, to evolve towards happiness. If she had been truly *avant garde,* if she had been less Min Vague.

Murmurations

The lawn had been partly shaded by the house when the boy started digging, but by mid-morning he was under the full blast of the sun. He turned the peak of his cap to the back but still he could feel the skin on his neck burning, so he got a towel out of his kit bag and draped it around his shoulders. The garden behind the old sandstone house had been allowed to go a bit wild, but it was still lovely. The boy thought it a pity the lawn was being cleared, but the owners wanted to do away with mowing, they wanted to minimise their water use. Sheltered by ivy-clad stone walls, the garden was like one in a book he'd once read, though the title eluded him. Also, it reminded him of home – that overgrown plot beyond the ruined potting sheds. The boy leaned for a moment on the shovel, staring into the shadowed back corner of the garden, and something passing through his mind caused him to lower his face, and slowly rub a hand across his eyes.

The boy's boss, Len Robsart, had delivered him to the site with a selection of shovels. There was another job in progress on the far side of the city, which Len would tackle alone, and at the end of the day he'd return to collect his apprentice. Len was a big, easy-going man, with a darkened front tooth and a slight limp from a digger accident during his own apprenticeship. When they had met, the boy had liked him on sight, judging him softer than his rough appearance suggested, and he had made up his mind to throw his full effort into working for Len.

A sod cutter could have dug up the lawn in a morning, whereas it was going to take the boy the best part of a week. It wasn't that Len was mean, but he had given a fixed quote and he was anxious to maximise profit. He had explained how in summer the landscaping business went quiet, and that it would pick up again after the holidays.

As the boy marked out the next square of turf with the shovel blade, a curtain in one of the windows twitched. When he and Len had arrived, a woman had emerged from the house to hand over a key to the side gate. She was rumpled-looking, all edges, with sharp cheekbones, and strands of grey in her hair that she hadn't bothered to dye; she was wearing faded jeans, and a floral blouse fastened at the top with a safety pin. Because of the missing button the boy had thought she might be the cleaning woman, but after she had gone back inside, Len said it was her house, and that her husband was a doctor.

All through the morning, as he hacked at the matted grass with his shovel, he sensed her watching from inside the house. Eventually he looked up to see her standing on the small porch off what looked like the kitchen.

"There's a jug of iced water," she said. "Take a break."

Obediently, he pressed the shovel into the turf with his boot, dropped his gloves beside it and crossed to the porch. Two steps up; it was shaded with a vine. He hesitated, sweaty and awkward, blistered hands dangling helplessly.

"You can come up," she said.

On a small wicker table, the doctor's wife had set out a water jug and a glass, and a bottle of sunscreen. On either side were two wicker chairs.

She gestured towards the sunscreen. "I thought ... in case you forgot to bring some," she said.

Her voice sounded full of fog, like she had a cold. Close up, her face had a strained look, and her eyelids were red and puffy: he wondered if she'd been crying. He peeled off his cap and stepped up onto the porch. She poured water without touching the glass, ice cubes tinkling as they tumbled over the rim of the jug – he thought it a lovely sound, and already felt cooler.

"Well, I'll let you sit and catch your breath," she said, and as he stammered out his thanks she backed through the door and disappeared into the house.

He took the chair furthest from the kitchen door and reached for the glass of water. Small birds darted among the vine leaves overhanging the porch roof; he could see their flickering shapes in the shadows cast across the painted verandah boards. When the jug was empty he squeezed sunscreen into his palm and rubbed it over the back of his neck, then stroked the residue over his nose and cheeks. Inside the house someone had turned on the television, a sit-com with wave after wave of fake laughter.

Next day he took a broad-brimmed hat he'd found hanging on a peg in Len's shed, and filled an old soft drink bottle with water. At the house he unpacked the shovels, and his kitbag, and set his water bottle in the shade. He wanted the woman to know he wouldn't be putting her to any trouble while he was digging out her lawn. When Len drove away, the boy turned and glanced towards the house. It looked empty, though he couldn't have said what was different. As the day wore on there was no sight of the woman, and by the time Len picked him up he'd concluded there was no one at home.

The following day, at around midday, the woman came out of the house carrying a cardboard box. She walked past him and disappeared around the side of the house; he guessed she was putting something in the shed. Uncertain and embarrassed, he could feel himself flush: should he have offered to carry the box for her? Would that be considered polite, or pushy? He had no idea how city people expected him to behave. Furious at his own ignorance, he resumed digging, slicing the grass and swinging the shovel with an almost manic energy. The woman returned and went into the house, and after a while she appeared on the porch and invited him to stop for a cold drink.

She was a little jittery, he noticed, but her eyes, two sapphire chips, gave off sparks.

"Your dad should've got in a machine to clear the grass," she said. "Digging in this heat's likely to kill you."

"I'll be okay," he said. "And Len's not my dad."

"Oh?" She stared at him for a moment, then waved him towards one of the chairs and disappeared into the house. When she reappeared she was carrying an empty glass – to his consternation she sat on the second chair and filled her glass from the water jug.

What's your name?" she said.

"It's Arthur, Ma'am."

"I should have realised." She smiled, and her glance seemed to take in the whole of him – from his too-big nose and his freckled ear lobes below the dark thatch of hair, to his lanky body that was only not awkward to him when he was asleep. "You don't look at all like you're related, you and Mister Robsart," she said.

He sipped his water in silence, allowed an ice cube to melt on his tongue.

"Where're you from, Arthur?"

He went to say he was from the city now, because the old life had shut behind him like a back door slammed by the wind. Instead, he heard himself telling her he was from the island.

The surprise and curiosity in her voice sounded genuine. "Have your folks always lived there?"

Arthur shook his head. "I was raised in The Star," he said. "It's a children's home, The Star of Bethlehem."

The woman took a slow sip from her glass. "You seem to have left pretty young."

"Boys can't stay in the home once they turn fifteen," he said. "Girls can be older."

"That's rough on the boys. Have you been working long for Mr Robsart?"

"About six months," he said. "Ma'am, he isn't a bad boss, even if he didn't want to get in a sod cutter."

"Yes, well I suppose he knows his own business," the woman said, but all the energy had ebbed out of her and her voice had turned vague, as if suddenly she was thinking about something else. By the time he went and picked up his shovel he could hear the television going inside the house, the canned laughter of a comedy show.

Next morning the woman appeared on the porch almost as soon as Len's truck drove away. She sat in one of the wicker chairs, smoking and watching him dig. Around noon she went inside, and brought out the jug of iced water and a plate of sandwiches.

"Come on, Arthur, time to cool down."

When he stepped onto the verandah he saw that she had also brought out a tube of antiseptic cream, and a pair of white cotton gloves.

"I noticed you had blisters," she said. "You have to be careful they don't get infected."

Arthur was flushed from the sun, and from the effort of digging, and now he felt the stinging in his palms where the blisters had burst but it was like a warning siren went off inside him: it was good of her to put out the cream, but it scared him, too, this intimate observation by a stranger. Although if it hadn't been for Len's missus, he might have just accepted that the doctor's wife had a kind heart. Arthur squirmed away from the thought of Barbara Robsart – the sly liberties she took when her husband's back was turned.

But his immediate problem was that he didn't know what he was supposed to do with the cotton gloves. Somehow the woman must have divined this, because she picked them up off the table and handed them to him.

"Wear these inside your heavy gloves," she said. "They'll cut down the rubbing, give the blisters a chance to heal."

He nodded warily, and folded the gloves into a pocket.

The woman filled his glass, and offered the plate of sandwiches. "Do me a favour and eat something," she said. "I love to feed people, and no one ever comes around for a meal anymore."

Her speech was a tiny bit odd today, he thought, but maybe that was just him, and his nerves that had been set aflutter when Len's wife intruded into his thoughts. His hand shook as he reached for a sandwich, but the woman appeared not to notice. She had begun to tell him a story about herself.

"Like you, I left home young," she said, "because after my mum died, my father remarried."

She hunched forward in her chair, and Arthur saw that there were bruises on the insides of her arms, and that her unpainted nails were chewed. He noticed, too, the habit she had of clasping one hand with the other, like she was holding her own hand for comfort.

"Marcy was a terrible woman, but he wouldn't hear a word against her," she said. "Of course, she was sweet as pie all the time he was there, but as soon as he walked out the door she would start tormenting me."

Arthur's mouth filled with saliva. Missus Robsart had come up behind him that morning as he stood drinking his tea in Len's kitchen – Len had gone outside to the shed; they could hear him banging about in there, cursing over a misplaced saw. When Arthur had put down his tea cup and turned from the sink, she had caught his hand and squeezed it against her ample breast. He had felt the thump of her heart, and her nipple, hard as a peanut, had rubbed against his palm. Even now he could feel the place where it had pressed, and he writhed with the memory of it, and with feelings for which he could not find words.

Sweating, vaguely nauseous, he drained the glass of water the woman had poured for him.

"I used to record in my journal what Marcy said and did. One day while I was at school she found where I'd hidden the book, and she put it in the fire. When I told my father he said, 'Now Erris, your mother wouldn't do a thing like that. Don't tell dirty lies!'" With her lips pressed tight, she shrugged. "So he beat me to show Marcy he was on her side. But it wasn't the beating made me decide to leave, it was because he'd called Marcy my mother."

"How old were you?" The question slipped from Arthur's mouth before he could stop it, and he was shocked that he'd dared to ask her anything: him, the landscape gardener's labourer, questioning her, the doctor's wife.

"Fifteen," she said. "Like you, Arthur."

"I've turned sixteen," he said, unable to keep from his voice a shy note of pride.

It was the same pride he felt in the inches he'd grown this last year, and in his arms that were no longer soft as a pair of sausages but muscled and strong. Secretly, too, he was proud of the fine dark down that shadowed his upper lip, the private parts that were nested in soft black curls. Somehow, this physical growth, the transformation of his body from child to man, felt like the only thing he had ever entirely owned, the only thing that had ever been truly private. Yet it was this that Robsart's wife wished to steal.

"My stepmother kept huge aviaries," the woman said. "All kinds of small birds, she bred and sold them. She liked birds more than she liked people." Her hand shook as she refilled his glass, so that water splashed onto the plate of sandwiches, and over the wicker table.

He watched her rise and move towards the kitchen; she returned with a dish cloth. Arthur stared out over the garden while she mopped up the spill. When she'd finished she offered him the sandwiches again, and he took one to show goodwill.

"That day that I left," she said, "I opened all the cages. At first the birds didn't know what to do, so I ran from cage to cage, banging on the wire netting with a stick. Suddenly the air was thick with birds. It was more beautiful than you could ever imagine."

Arthur could imagine it all too well, and for the first time since he'd left the island he thought of the starlings massed at dusk in the winter trees behind the children's home. He remembered the rustle of their wings when they twisted in skeins over the fields, or swelled and contracted high above the cliffs, dark wave after dark wave, lifting and falling in a kind of dance. Sister Lucy had said it was a murmuration. He was still quite young, and he had thought the birds were showing him a sign, that there was something written in their fluid patterns. Probably he'd thought it was a message from his mum – all of them had been obsessed with their mothers – and he had wept bitter tears because he couldn't read it.

A few years later, when he was sick one time, he had looked down from a high window in the sanatorium just as the play bell rang and all the kids ran into the yard. In their dull grey overalls, with their dark, bobbed heads, they had exploded across the cobbled quad like small birds flocking. Their boots on the cobbles had sounded like the beating of wings; so swift were they that their separate shapes were blurred – it was a flow of bodies coming together and pulling apart, but always more of them together: a murmuration of children.

It had been wrong to send them out one by one. They should have gone into the world in groups, or at the very least in pairs; they'd have kept each other strong. He should write to Mother Stella Marie, tell her that going it alone was too hard after a crowded childhood. He wouldn't write, of course. But it made him feel better to think that he could.

Linnie's birthday would have been at the end of the summer. She'd have been seventeen. They had dreamed of finding a place together, and they'd laughed about not having to wrap newspaper around their shins to wade through the nettles behind the potting sheds to reach their private domain. And it was those hours he'd spent there with Linnie – their murmurs in the long grass, her mouth warm against his ear – which Len's missus was stealing from him too.

The worst of it was that he couldn't complain to Len. If Len believed him, he'd be shattered, because Arthur could tell that Len adored his wife. But his wife was not the woman Len believed – if he only knew. And from the way she looked into his eyes and smiled while she was touching him, that hard, mocking gleam, she knew for sure he couldn't tell Len.

To Arthur's horror, hot tears welled up and spilled down his cheeks. He sat as if frozen, the half-eaten sandwich still in his hand. Tears dripped down his neck, and the woman put down her drink.

"What is it?" she said.

But Arthur couldn't speak. It was Linnie he was crying for, and how the letter had come to say she'd fallen to her death from a window at that shirt factory they sent her to – a little bird that hadn't been able to fly. Well, maybe he was another one. Maybe that was the only way out for him.

Arthur's shoulders were shaking with the effort of holding himself in the chair; though he was blinded by tears he was aware of the woman going into the house, of her coming out again.

"Here," she said softly, "use this."

It was a tea cloth with a comforting, fresh-ironed smell. He pressed it to his eyes, blocking out the porch and the woman.

"If there's anything I can do," she said.

She hadn't touched him. And with his face buried in her cloth he heard himself bawling out everything he'd been holding in, about growing up with people always around him, and now being cast adrift, about Linnie, and about Missus Robsart, and that one time she'd bailed him up while Len was out, him like a rabbit and her like a weasel, and how part of him had wanted to escape and another part had wanted to grab her and throw her down and show her that he was stronger than she thought. And how he could never tell Len. He even told her his theory about being sent out in groups, like birds. But by the time he'd got to the birds, a new and terrifying thought had occurred to Arthur: what if the woman took upon herself to inform his boss?

He dropped the cloth into his lap and looked at her in a kind of pleading silence.

"It's all right," she said quickly, "I won't say anything to Mister Robsart. But you need to get away, Arthur. You have to find other work. You know that, don't you?"

He nodded. But it wasn't that easy. Even a woman like her who had left home at fifteen had probably forgotten what it was like, living from one pay to the next. At the end of the week, when Len gave him his wages, once he'd settled his board there was so little left over.

The woman went inside and returned with a mug of tea. "I guessed you'd take it with milk and two spoonfuls of sugar," she said. "Am I right?"

After he'd drunk the tea he felt better, and got up to go and dig the last of the lawn. When he heard Len's truck coming, he splashed his face with water from his water bottle and mopped up with the old t-shirt. He hoped he didn't look like he'd been crying, hoped Len would be pleased that he'd finished off the grass. Tomorrow they would load the cut turf onto the truck, and then they'd be done. Someone else was coming to lay the paving.

That night, he washed the cotton gloves she had given him and hung them to dry. He'd return them to her, though she probably would throw them away. Arthur wished he could think of some way to thank her for her kindness, but nothing occurred to him. He would give them to her as they were leaving, so that if it was the wrong thing to have done he'd be going anyway.

The next afternoon, with Len on site, there wasn't much opportunity for him to approach the woman. Luckily, she came out onto the porch just as Len went to relieve himself against the back fence. Arthur took the gloves from his kit bag and walked over to her.

"In case you wanted them back," he said. "I washed them."

"Oh! You shouldn't have worried." She looked past him, and then, seeing that Len was busy, she reached into the pocket of her skirt and pulled out an envelope.

"Don't open it until later," she said, and the sudden smile she gave him lit her face, so that he saw all the sharp-edged beauty that was still there under the greying hair, the reddened eyelids. "Good luck, Arthur," she murmured in her foggy voice. "Go well!" And she turned away before he could say anything.

Len was whistling as he walked up the yard. Arthur sensed that the woman didn't want him to know about the envelope, so he slipped it inside his shirt and wandered over to the truck.

"Good to go?" Len said.

The woman waved from the porch as Len eased the truck down the drive. Later, in his room, Arthur opened the envelope. Inside, he found a letter; it was sealed and stamped, and addressed to Delia someone-or-other. She had written in pencil on the back: *please post.* But the biggest shock was that the outer envelope contained a thousand dollars in cash, and a note, addressed to him, scribbled on a page torn from a lined note book: *Fly away, Arthur. Fly far, be free. Erris.*

Around the edges of the paper, cloud shapes were filled with dozens of small, dark, pencilled birds.

Paper Boats

Amanda has sent a short story to *The New Yorker*. On the walk to the post office she'd felt purposeful, but the moment the envelope slips from her fingers into the box she wishes she could wrench it back. Writers she reveres have been published in *The New Yorker*, literary greats like William Trevor and Alice Munro, and, going back a bit, the sharp, the stylish, the tragic, Maeve Brennan. What on earth was she thinking! Amanda stares into the dark slot that has swallowed her story, and as always at the point of letting go she thinks of how the word 'submission' suggests humiliation, suggests a helpless yielding.

"Forget you've posted it," she tells herself sternly. And in a day or two she will forget for quite large chunks of time. But just at the moment, she is stricken.

"It's a story that needed to be told," she says, and turns her back on the post box.

The idea had come from her neighbour, Magda Woźniak. Amanda and Magda live in the two rundown villas bequeathed to them on the deaths of their respective parents, old, high-ceilinged houses, like most others in the surrounding streets.

Once occupied by migrant families, they had been affordable only because they had fallen out of favour for being difficult to heat, and in constant need of repair. But as the older generation gradually died out, so the suburb has been colonised by young professionals, couples who spend their weekdays in city offices, and their weekends renovating.

In their un-renovated homes, Magda and Amanda are the only residents on their street who remember their Menick and Woźniak parents; they are almost the only residents who remember when kids played hopscotch on the pavements, and the front yards were filled with tomato plants. On Sunday afternoons they like to sit together for a few hours, drinking coffee and gossiping. When it's Amanda's turn to host Magda she bakes a carrot cake, or in summer she will make a strawberry and rhubarb pie because it is Magda's favourite, and it pleases Amanda to watch her neighbour eat – Magda, who is as thin and straight as a clothes peg, works as a contract cleaner, and Amanda worries that she still smokes, that she doesn't eat properly.

The things Magda sees and hears and is asked to clean up after often provide the substance of their Sunday chats. Amanda has never felt compelled to write about anything she's heard, until Magda told how she'd been sent to clear a house of the belongings of a woman who'd died. They'd been sitting on the back verandah to catch the last of the sun, the street quiet but for the distant drone of a lawn mower.

"The husband couldn't bring himself to touch anything she'd owned, which is common enough," Magda said. "Usually it's because they're not coping with the grief."

But this husband had been different.

"He'd loathed his wife. I felt it as soon as I walked through their front door."

"How could you tell?" Amanda poured coffee while Magda lit a cigarette.

"There was an atmosphere you couldn't miss. Anyway, it turned out that they had slept in separate rooms, and before he took me into her bedroom," Magda paused, and her pencilled brows shot skywards, "he pulled on a pair of surgical gloves."

"To go into her bedroom? How very odd!"

Magda shrugged. "He was a doctor, so I suppose he had a ready supply of those gloves."

"He didn't wear a gown and mask, did he?"

"No." Magda said. "But I'll tell you this – he seemed to be holding his breath in that room. It was as if he didn't want to breathe, just in case there was some air left in there that might have been exhaled by his wife."

They sat in silence, Magda blowing cigarette smoke out the side of her mouth so that it drifted away from where Amanda sat, and across the garden.

"I will say," said Magda, "that it was very close in that room. It had been shut up tight as a tomb. The first thing I did once he'd gone was to open the window."

Later, when she'd been bagging up the woman's clothes, Magda had found miniature bottles of vodka pushed down into the toes of shoes, and hidden in the pockets of coats and dresses hanging in the wardrobe."

"Most were empty, but one or two were still full. I expect she'd forgotten where she'd put them."

A question had floated into Amanda's mind then: what if the husband had worn gloves so as not to leave fingerprints in his wife's bedroom? If the room was being cleared it was not a crime scene, so her death had not been deemed suspicious. But what if he had caused that death? What if he'd got away with it, but was still being careful, just in case?

"How did she die?" Amanda asked.

Magda held out her mug for a refill. "He never said. Some alcohol related illness, you would think."

Amanda had felt a quiver of unease. What if the bottles had been planted; what if the wife hadn't ever been a drinker? It was the gloves that bothered her: they were so clinical, so calculated.

"What was he like, the husband?"

Magda thought for a moment. "He was … like a heron," she said slowly, "all legs and beak. Sad looking, I suppose you could say, and scrupulously polite." But Magda, picking up cake crumbs with her fingertips, which, like her hands, were red from scrubbing, and from contact with cleaning chemicals, had one more surprise.

"There was a nursery room," she said. "The wallpaper and matching curtains were yellow and white – sunflowers and bunnies. There was nothing else. No furniture, nothing in the built-in wardrobe. But when I lifted the rug to sweep underneath, I found something." She had reached into her bag and pulled out a paper boat. "I kept it to show you."

Magda set it on the table beside their coffee mugs, and they stared at it: a tiny boat made of paper torn from a lined notebook. On the prow, its name: *Erris*.

"Look, there's more." With her reddened fingers, Magda gently unfolded the paper sail. Inside, pencilled letters that seemed about to fade before their eyes:

I was never mad

"Shouldn't you take this to the police?" Amanda said.

"They'd laugh their legs off," Magda said.

The flattened paper, with its creases, looked like something you would find blowing along the street, and yet its pencilled message rushed at Amanda; it entered her chest as a formless, aching beat. She picked up her mug and steadied herself with a mouthful of the strong black coffee.

When Magda had gone Amanda had thought she probably wouldn't write about it – after all, it seemed like the start of a crime story and she wasn't a crime writer. But then neither was Alice Munro, yet her stories teemed with violent deeds. So Amanda had sat down at her writing desk and allowed herself to imagine Alice beside her, guiding her hand and thoughts, and when the story was finished she had thought it one of her best.

Amanda has other stories out on submission. Her life is one of writing, and waiting, and while she waits she must maintain her hope, while ignoring the obliterating silence that emanates from the places she has submitted work to. The silence of editors and publishers is matched only by the silence of the grave, but then occasionally a note of encouragement flutters in, a small white ghostly bird that lands chirping on her desk. It was after one such message that she had converted the garden shed into her writing room.

There have been successes; stories published in anthologies, one or two in the company of well-known authors. A reviewer once described her prose as 'finely tempered and meditative', and a literary agent had read that review and made contact. The agent had suggested that Amanda expand her story into a novel, and she had tried – draft after draft. But the agent had wanted a racier style, and eventually it had become clear to both of them that Amanda couldn't write in that vein. She didn't even read the sort of books the agent was suggesting she write.

Walking away from the mail box in which her story, in its crisp white envelope, floats in the first dark pool of its outward journey, Amanda turns towards the station. Dry leaves tumbled by the wind make a scratching sound that sets her nerves on edge. She wonders whether William Trevor ever becomes discouraged, or Alice. Surely they are both so well published that they are past the point where they could ever feel dejected. Poor Maeve Brennan, though, for all her wit and skill, she had touched rock bottom. Maeve's editor at *The New Yorker* had been William Maxwell. Imagine! Maxwell is another writer Amanda reveres, and a beautiful human being, too, by all accounts. She saw a picture of him once in which his face had seemed to shine with goodness. To deserve such an editor, a writer must be exceptional. On her better days, Amanda tells herself that anyone can dream.

In the railway station entrance, a woman with mad bright eyes and straggling grey hair jiggles a placard on a pole: *Christ is Coming and He will Repay Unbelievers with Affliction!* She thrusts a leaflet at Amanda, who accepts it and shoves it into her bag, noting that the woman is no older than she is and might even be a year or two younger. It is then that Amanda feels herself sinking, as helpless and as doomed as when she had drifted into the deep end at the swimming baths as a child, while her mother sat on the grass, engrossed in a book. If it hadn't been for someone else's mother jumping in and hauling her out she'd have drowned. But who will haul her out now? Her story is on its way to one of the world's iconic magazines.

On the train, searching in her handbag for a mint, Amanda takes out the crumpled leaflet. What affliction, she wonders, is in store for her? She scans it to see whether there is a date for the predicted Rapture, because with luck it will arrive before the *New Yorker* receives her submission. It will certainly come before they respond. Then again, you never know: her story is compact, and sometimes an editor is desperate to fill a small space, though never, she suspects, an editor at *The New Yorker*.

Amanda returns the leaflet to her bag – she is not a sharp enough writer for *The New Yorker*. Not yet. And if the world does not end and save her, she can only pray that whoever reads it will not write a cruel letter. Because it takes her so long to recover from the shame of failure, which in some twisted way is like the creeping shame she has felt after rough treatment from one or two men she has known, men who are no longer in her life. But why, she wonders, do women accept the blame that shame implies? Why do writers? *I was never mad:* damn it, what *had* happened to that woman!

From the suburban station where she alights, she will catch a bus to where her daughter lives. Amanda is hazy on the details of bus numbers and timetables, but when the bus arrives she checks with the driver, and climbs on board.

If she had been able to satisfy that literary agent, her life would have been different. Friends would not roll their eyes when she refuses to lunch because it cuts into her working day. Lizbie would be proud of her. There would have been money to fix up the house, and she could have afforded a car. But lately Amanda is full of vague aches and pains; the literary skill she aspires to takes time to develop, and at least she hasn't poured precious years into books that will be read once and discarded. What she yearns for in her writing is to hit one true note. A note that will make sense of something, perhaps of everything, a note that will crack the obliterating silence, once and for all.

She suspects that the story she has just written might have hit that note. If she has been able to capture what she felt when she first heard it from Magda – the sealed room, those gloves, that tiny message, and her sense of something hidden that needed to be uncovered, something dark and rotten, even evil, which has masqueraded as normality.

At the last moment, Amanda recognises the row of shops on the corner of Lizbie's street and she presses the stop button. When the bus lurches to a halt she moves to the front.

"Have a good day, lady," the driver says as she steps down.

Ignoring his peeved tone, Amanda thanks him, and sets off towards the sea.

She has brought Lizbie a jar of raw organic honey; she has brought pecans, and almonds, and a block of beautiful white nougat with pistachios. Lizbie has grown increasingly haggard in the years since her husband's death; she looks a little like the woman who handed Amanda the leaflet outside the station, only younger. Amanda reminds herself that there have been times when she, too, let herself go down. Widows do, and then after a while they pull themselves up. The difference is that she'd had a small child to care for, and it's this that worries her about Lizbie – there seems so little to tether her to life. Every Monday afternoon, Amanda takes the train and the bus to bring whatever small treats she can gather. She would come more often if Lizbie would let her.

Amanda remembers her daughter as a newborn with the shock of hair that had suggested her name, because of Hardy's poem: *'And, Lizbie Browne, Who else had hair bay-red as yours, Or flesh so fair'*. She remembers her skipping cracks in the pavement, and then as a stroppy teen, impossible to deal with once she was on the pill.

At Lizbie's gate she pauses, steadies herself with a few deep breaths before turning in.

Months pass without news of her submissions. But Amanda is engrossed in reading and re-reading Maeve Brennan's *The Springs of Affection* as if a painstaking progress through its pages will show her how to emulate Maeve's stripped yet devastating prose. By the time *The Springs of Affection* first appeared in print Maeve Brennan had spent time in a mental hospital. But could you ever guess that from reading her masterpiece? Apparently, Maeve had thought people were trying to poison her by putting cyanide in her toothpaste.

I was never mad: what failure, what shame, what guilt had caused the doctor's wife to fold a tiny boat and write inside its sail?

Amanda has begun another story; it's set in the year following her husband's death. After Joe's brain tumour she had sunk to her lowest, yet she'd done her best to look after Lizbie. The form of the story is slowly coming to her, and she has put the *Do Not Disturb* sign on the door of her writing room. But on Thursday afternoon she is interrupted by a furious knocking. When she is slow to respond, Magda shouts, "Are you in there?"

Amanda is still half in the world of her story when she opens the door.

"Sorry," Magda waves a newspaper, "but will you look at this."

She opens the paper on Amanda's desk, and points at a black and white photograph in which a woman gazes unsmiling over her left shoulder at the camera. Her hair is scraped back into a ponytail, exposing a face in which the mouth is dark with lipstick, the eyebrows curved like the wings of a bird. "It's that doctor's wife."

Together they stare at it, and as the woman stares back at them Magda says, "The police are investigating her death."

"Why now?" Amanda says.

"Something turned up," says Magda. "It seems she had written to an old friend right before she died. The friend had moved around a lot, but when the letter finally found her, she took it to the police."

Police have opened an investigation into the death of Mrs Erris Cleary ...

"Was she buried?"

"Cremated."

How, then, was anything to be proved? Amanda leans closer to study the face – sharp, grave, alert, intelligent; the woman's pose, her severely pulled back hair, remind her of Maeve Brennan. People have been tried for murder even without a body; there have been famous cases.

Magda says, "I should have gone to the police."

"They'll want to speak to you now," Amanda says. "You still have that paper boat, don't you?"

Magda pulls a face, and shakes her head.

"Even so, we both saw it."

"I'll go tomorrow morning, before work," says Magda. "There's that local police station near the hospital."

"If you like, I'll come with you."

Tossing and turning in the early hours, Amanda wonders whether she should write to *The New Yorker* and withdraw her story. She wonders why, if that doctor had killed his wife, he would run the risk of bringing in a contract cleaner? Because he had wanted someone, a random stranger, to witness the wardrobe full of bottles!

In Amanda's story there are two endings. Without an autopsy it could be the same in real life. The doctor's wife might have hidden those bottles, or they might have been planted; her husband might have killed her for reasons of his own, or he might only have hated her alcoholism. But then why put on *gloves* to go into her room? If the husband never harmed her, Amanda would like him to explain the gloves.

Amanda rises early, and a pain in her hip that is new sets up a protest as she shuffles to the kitchen to fill the kettle. By the time Magda arrives she is dressed and ready, still tired, but moving more freely. Exercise eases the stiffness: Amanda knows this, yet she is a reluctant walker.

"I wish I hadn't thrown out that boat," Magda says. "I feel so stupid."

"You weren't to know." Amanda gathers her purse and keys. "How could anyone be expected to?"

They set off under a clouded sky, along streets not yet clogged by rush hour traffic. This would be a good time of day to walk, Amanda thinks, if she could ever get motivated.

The police station has a sealed look, and Magda scans its blank windows with anxious eyes. "Do you think they'll take us seriously?"

They mount worn slate steps, and push through a heavy door into a waiting room. There are scuffed white walls, and a lofty ceiling; light flares in a trio of windows high above their heads. Aside from the two of them, an old lady with bandaged legs dozes under a wall heater, and a hazel-haired young woman perches on a bench seat; she glances up at them, her eyes a wounded blue.

There is no one behind the glassed-in counter.

"At least my first job's not 'til ten," Magda says.

They sit side by side, and as Amanda shifts her left buttock to ease her hip she marvels at how the young woman's spine never touches the back of the bench. What it must be like – the absence of pain, and no inkling that one day that will change. The young woman brings out a string of beads from her bag; they are lumpy and dark, with a little chain and a cross, a rosary; she cups them in her hands for a minute, and then puts them away.

A female police officer appears at the counter, and the young woman rises from the bench with a bird-like grace. The old lady still dozes, and Amanda wonders whether she is only there for the heater.

"Maybe we'll be next," says Magda.

A sudden flood of light at the windows washes over them, illuminating Magda's small plain face with its sun-damaged skin and smoker's wrinkles. A surge of love for her friend catches in Amanda's throat: who'd have ever thought they would get this old. She turns to watch the young woman, whose body is poised at a tentative slant as she speaks to the policewoman. She nods, and hands a yellow envelope across the counter, and after a minute or two, a door Amanda has not noticed slides open, and the young woman walks through it and disappears.

Amanda thinks of her story in its envelope, slithering into the dark of the post box. Life is full of hidden doors and unexpected openings. She will not withdraw her work. It might be wishful thinking, but her gut feeling is that this one will find a decent home – maybe not *The New Yorker,* but somewhere that means something. If at last she has hit that one true note it must be allowed to ring, it must be allowed to shatter the silence.

Acknowledgements

Murmurations is not set in a specific city, or country, but in the daunting urban landscapes painted by the American artist Edward Hopper. Noted for his reticence and habitual silence, Hopper's flat, saturated colours, his erasing of detail, produced pictures in which absence is as compelling and eloquent as presence. Each of these stories began as a response to one of Hopper's paintings, and while the original prompts are no longer necessary to the novella that grew out of them, the works that provided the inspiration are, in order of appearance: *Automat* (1927); *Hotel Window* (1956); *Stairway* (circa 1925); *Summer Evening* (1947); *Room in New York* (1940); *Morning Sun* (1952); *Summer in the City* (1949); *Woman in the Sun* (1961).

I am grateful for the continuing support of the Department of English and Creative Writing at the University of Adelaide, where I am a Visiting Research Fellow. Gratitude to the shakers and movers at Spinifex Press: Susan Hawthorne, Renate Klein, and Pauline Hopkins, and to all those who work behind the scenes. Thanks too, to my agent Fran Moore, and to my indefatigable friend Gay Lynch, for her fierce encouragement, perceptive reading, and generous responses. I am indebted to Annette Willis for the beautiful book on Edward Hopper that allowed me to study his paintings as prints rather than on a screen. Finally, love and gratitude to Christopher and Rafael Lefevre without whom I would be lonelier than a Hopper painting.

Other fiction titles available from Spinifex Press

The Happiness Glass
Carol Lefevre

But what did teenage girls in country towns want with Latin and French and art? What use would it be to them?

The literary longings of a studious girl born into a working class family, hot afternoons in a dust-plain Wilcannia schoolhouse; the temptation to stay, and the perils of breaking free — *The Happiness Glass* reflects complex griefs in the life of Lily Brennan.

Lily's story allows the author to navigate some of the difficulties of memoir, and out of its bittersweet blend of real, remembered, and imagined life, the portrait of a writer gradually emerges.

In fiction that forms around a core of memory, life writing that acknowledges the elusiveness of truth, Carol Lefevre has written a remarkable, risk-taking book that explores questions of homesickness, infertility, adoption, and family estrangement, in Lily Brennan's life, and in her own.

"… These scenes are worthy of Patrick White. There are many pleasures in this short, cunningly crafted, deeply felt book, not the least of which is consistently good writing."
—Susan Varga, *Australian Book Review*

ISBN: 9781925581638

Locust Girl: A Lovesong
Merlinda Bobis

Winner 2016 – Christina Stead Prize for Fiction,
NSW Premer's Literary Awards
Shortlisted: 2016 ACT Book of the Year Award
Philippine National Book Award for Best Novel in English

Most everything has dried up: water, the womb, even the love among lovers. Hunger is rife, except across the border. Nine-year-old Amadea survives the bombing of her village to wake ten years later with a locust embedded in her brow. She journeys to the border, which has cut the human heart. Can she repair it with the story of a small life? This is the Locust Girl's dream, her lovesong.

"… a book that can be read with pleasure for its language alone, and which subtly and surely subverts the status quo. Bobis messes with our minds, in the very best way."

—Lucy Sussex, *The Sydney Morning Herald*

"It's allegorically pertinent not just to the question of refugees but also to how the future might play out if climate change is as disastrous as some of the modelling suggests."

—Ed Wright, *The Australian*

ISBN: 9781742199627

The Floating Garden
Emma Ashmere

Sydney, 1926, and the residents of the tight-knit Milsons Point community face imminent homelessness: the construction of the harbour bridge spells the demolition of their homes. Ellis Gilbey, landlady by day, gardening writer by night, is set to lose everything. Only her belief in the book she is writing, and the hopes of a garden of her own, allow her to fend off despair. This beautiful debut novel evokes the hardships and the glories of the 1920s and tells the little-known story of those who faced upheaval because of the famous bridge.

"*The Floating Garden* is a fine example how fiction can be useful in expanding our understanding of the past ... I enthusiastically recommend this book to other readers, especially those who care about Sydney, and those interested in a new type of historical fiction."

—M.D. Brady, *Me, You, and Books*

ISBN: 9781742199368

Dark Matters: A novel
Susan Hawthorne

When Desi inherits her aunt Kate's house in Brunswick she begins to read the contents of the boxes in the back room. She discovers a hidden life, one which could not be shared with Kate's family.

Among the papers are records of arrest, imprisonment and torture at the hands of an unknown group who persecute her for her sexuality and activism. Scraps of memoir, family history and poems complete this fragmented story.

Can Desi find Mercedes? The woman Kate has loved so much. Mercedes, who had escaped from Pinochet's Chile. Where is she and can she help unravel Kate's story?

"*Dark Matters* is a transformative tour de force; lyrical as Sappho and revolutionary as Wittig in *Les Guérillères*."
—Roberta Arnold, *Sinister Wisdom*

"This is a book of underworlds and infernos, places of execution, practices of erasure and sites of desire. It documents the practicalities of attempting to break lesbian cultures woman by woman, finger by finger and story by story. Against such violence Hawthorne offers poetry as activism, as remedy, as mode of repair. *Dark Matters* is a meteoroid. When it hits, it will make a different world of you."
—Hayley Singer, *Cordite Poetry Review*

ISBN: 9781925581089

Symphony for the Man
Sarah Brill

1999. Winter. Bondi. Harry's been on the streets so long he could easily forget what time is. So Harry keeps an eye on it. Every morning. Then he heads to the beach to chat with the gulls. Or he wanders through the streets in search of food, clothes, Jules. When the girl on the bus sees him, lonely and cold in the bus shelter that he calls home, she thinks about how she can help. She decides to write a symphony for him.

So begins a poignant and gritty tale of homelessness and shelter, of the realities of loneliness and hunger, and of the hopes and dreams of those who often go unnoticed on our streets. This is the story of two outcasts—one a young woman struggling to find her place in an alien world, one an older man seeking refuge and solace from a life in tatters. It is also about the transformative power of care and friendship, and the promise of escape that music holds.

An uplifting and heartbreaking story that demands empathy. Amid the struggles to belong and fit in, we are reminded that small acts of kindness matter. And big dreams are possible.

"Music transforms lives in an intricate symphony of grit and grime that is delicately infiltrated by flourishes of magic realism. Simple, rippling, meditative prose details a miracle of kindness. This strangely filmic novel makes its stealthy way into the reader's heart."

—Carmel Bird

ISBN: 9781925950069

Lillian's Eden
Cheryl Adam

In *Lillian's Eden*, debut novelist Cheryl Adam takes the reader to Australian rural post-war life through the life of a family struggling to survive. With their farm destroyed by fire, Lillian agrees to the demands of her philandering, violent husband to move to the coastal town of Eden to help look after his Aunt Maggie. Juggling caring for her children and two households, Lillian finds an unlikely ally and friend in the feisty, eccentric Aunt Maggie who lives next door.

"*Lillian's Eden* has a rather classic feel to it, harking back to life during the 1950s in rural Australia. In many ways, it is reminiscent of *The Dressmaker* and *Cloudstreet*, with its element of the ridiculous that only comes with this type of nostalgic Australian fiction. Unflinchingly honest, this is a novel that will have you in stitches from laughter while stealing your breath away with its emotional intensity."
—Theresa Smith, Theresa Smith Writes Blog

"*Lillian's Eden* is a garden full of stolen roses, family secrets and ambivalence. It's also home to one very attractive snake. I couldn't stop reading till I found who got cast out."
—Kristin Henry

ISBN: 9781925581676

*If you would like to know more about
Spinifex Press, write to us for a free catalogue, visit our
website or email us for further information
on how to subscribe to our monthly newsletter.*

Spinifex Press
PO Box 105
Mission Beach QLD 4852
Australia

www.spinifexpress.com.au
women@spinifexpress.com.au